In the heart of the Imperial Stars, past and future collide, as ghosts converge in battle for a fortuneteller's soul . . . on Port Destiny Station.

Luxi Emery was perfectly happy with her position as the receptionist for Armored Media Corp. Then her hidden talent for seeing the future awakened — and exposed a blackmailing con-artist haunted by a malevolent ghost. It was a lose-lose situation, and Luxi had only a single shred of hope.

Her future awaits on Port Destiny Station. A future intertwined with Amun, the handsome diplomatic telepath, and Leto, a ghost-haunted cyborg with very human carnal appetites. If they can resolve a few . . . intimate . . .details. Yet a darker future chases Luxi: they are not alone, and Leto is not the only hungry ghost.

Publisher's Note: This book contains explicit sexual content, graphic language, and situations that some readers may find objectionable: Anal play/intercourse, mild BDSM elements, menage (m/m/f), and homoerotic sexual situations (m/m).

Fortune's Star
Copyright © 2019 Morgan Hawke
ISBN: 978-1-4874-2636-1
Cover art by Martine Jardin

Published by eXtasy Books Inc or
Devine Destinies, an imprint of eXtasy Books Inc

Look for us online at:
www.eXtasybooks.com or www.devinedestinies.com

Fortune's Star
Interstellar Service and Discipline Book 1
A Tale from the Imperial Stars

By

Morgan Hawke

PROLOGUE

Armored Media Corporation
Estrella City, Temperance Prime

Luxi smiled as the data from the feed jacked into the base of her skull flowed smoothly through her internal computational array. The upgrade had been well worth the credits. The department's incoming and outgoing communications data was barely touching her conscious thoughts with not one trace of lag-time.

She turned her face to the tall windows right by her desk and peered out over the city's vista. Sunlight gleamed on the towers and spires of Uppercity's business district. Below her, two-man gliders and private sedan cruisers wove around massive freight hovers as they zipped along the traffic-filled airways.

Musing on the different levels of speeding air traffic, she ran her fingers lightly over her hair, making sure that the silver clip was still securely fastened. She didn't need her rolled and coiled waist-length hair unraveling and getting caught on the data jack. As curly as her hair was, the bright red strands had a nasty habit of wrapping tight around the feed wire. She utterly refused to cut it, not when it was her best feature, so keeping it tightly bound was her only option.

The entry door chimed gently then slid to the side, opening with a soft hiss. A tall businessman stalked in from the outer hallway.

Luxi stared at the tall man filling her tiny receptionist

1

alcove and felt every hair on her body rise. Her throat tightened for no good reason whatsoever. "Welcome to Armored Media Corp." Her voice came out breathless.

There was something terribly wrong with him.

He didn't *look* odd. In fact, he might have been considered handsome. He had strong clean-shaven features, and his shoulder-length sable hair was neatly trimmed. Broad shoulders filled out his simple but sedately expensive fawn overcoat with no sign of the paunch that most Uppercity businessmen carried. The single-button chocolate dress suit he wore under his long coat was also understated, but the super-fine material and the tailored cut reeked of money.

She'd seen lots of businessmen dressed like this and quite a few from off-world that were dressed far more exotically. None of them had ever given her a case of the chills . . .

He turned to Luxi and smiled. "I'm here to see Gentle-fem Symposia?" He held out his data card.

And every instinct in Luxi's body screamed that she was in danger.

Luxi took the card very carefully so as not to make actual physical contact with his fingers. She swallowed. "One moment, please." She swiped it through the desktop scanner then routed his data to Gentle-fem Symposia's office. His information consisted of a single name, and that was it.

Vincent . . .

Luxi frowned. *He must be some kind of private consultant.* She handed the card back.

He turned away and stared at one of the tasteful, but boring prints on the cream wall by the inner door. Luxi was clearly beneath his notice, and that suited her just fine.

Mercy Symposia, Director of the Executables Department of Armored Media, strode briskly into the reception alcove from the inner door. As usual, she appeared conservatively professional with her dark blonde hair in an elegant upsweep, yet sleek in her tailored black suit-dress. Chin up and smiling, she took Vincent's outstretched hand. "I'm so glad you could see me on such short notice."

Vincent bowed over Gentle-fem Symposia's hand then released it. "I found an opening in my schedule that permitted."

Luxi transferred data while keeping half an eye on the pair. What was it that set her off? Very casually, she stood up to get a better look. She swept her hands down her sleek and less than expensive, but nicely tailored dove-gray business dress. She fiddled with a few folders on the upper ledge of her desk while trying not to look directly at either of them.

Mercy's smile faded as she spoke with the gentleman. The conversation sounded like any other business discussion, and yet she seemed nervous.

Vincent stood with casual deference and nodded in complete understanding. He spoke in mild and polite tones, but his smile seemed a tad sharp and his eyes . . . His black eyes . . .

Luxi focused her quiescent mental talent on what she was feeling, and it awakened within the deeps of her mind. Synchronicities, the lines of coincidence and possibility ruled by the decisions made in the here and now, clarified and stretched outward into bright skeins that created the warp and weft of potential futures. Her attention slid down the threads of prospect, decision, and chance that the unnerving man shared with her boss, seeking the future they would create . . .

She cringed. This man was a con-artist that preyed on fear. If Gentle-fem Symposia did business with him even once, her boss would never be rid of him.

Luxi turned away. If she said anything to her boss, she would have to tell Gentle-fem Symposia how she knew. She had no doubts that she would be believed. Psi-talents were not unknown. Most people showed some trace of telepathy or telekinetic ability, but strong talents were rare. And her talent was very reliable.

That was the problem.

Exposing the existence of her particular talent would cost Luxi her job. The ability to track potential futures was just too much for any company to deal with. No one wanted to know that someone else was privy to their business decisions before they even made them. It didn't matter to them that she wouldn't know if she didn't actually look. They were all so busy angling for an advantage over the next company; it wouldn't occur to them that *she* simply did not care.

But if she didn't say anything, Luxi would lose her job anyway. The company would not take kindly to Gentle-fem Symposia's embezzlement to feed this man's need for cash. The office would be closed for months during the investigation. Mercy would be indentured to the company for life, and her staff disbanded, including the receptionist.

Luxi's possible futures burned in the back of her mind. No matter what she chose, her future was no longer here in this office. There was nothing she could do to stem the tide. The real decisions were not in her hands. Once that man had entered Mercy's life, Luxi's future had been doomed. Keeping silent would not save her.

But Gentle-fem Symposia's gratitude might.

There was one slim chance that Luxi would not end up living in the under-city slums — but it was slim indeed.

Luxi shut down her holographic display, pulled out her data jack and set the communications switchboard on auto. *Damnit, I really liked this job!* She took a steadying breath and lifted her chin. "Ms. Symposia, that man cannot be trusted."

Mercy turned a sharp look Luxi's way. "Luxi, you have no idea what you're talking about, he's a monk."

A monk? Luxi swallowed but held her supervisor's gaze steadily. "Gentle-fem Symposia, with all due respect, he's a blackmailing con-artist."

Her supervisor frowned. "What?"

The man suddenly focused on Luxi. His black eyes narrowed. "Miss, do you know what you are saying?"

Luxi stared coldly into his eyes. "Yes, as a matter of fact, I do." Abruptly her small and secondary talent stirred within her. She had no grasp on it or control over it, the talent came and it went as it pleased. It wasn't particularly useful — all her little talent saw was the threads of the past–– and ghosts.

As she stared into Vincent's black eyes, her second talent suddenly opened wide and showed her why her skin was crawling.

Vincent was possessed by a second soul. It was staring straight at her from within his eyes with malignant intent. It was very dead and very hungry.

Vincent suddenly smiled. It wasn't pretty.

Luxi literally felt the ground move under her feet as her future abruptly reshaped itself.

Mercy Symposia's office was not particularly large, but it boasted a full wall of solid windows that overlooked the heart of the corporate district of Estrella City. Her broad desk was an understated work of art made of real imported Blackwood. Mercy tapped at her keyboard and frowned thoughtfully at her holographic display.

Luxi sat in the elegant back-curved chair before the desk with her hands folded quietly in her lap. She had been right. Mercy had not had any difficulty believing once she understood Luxi's odd talent. Fortunetellers were a dime a dozen, but none of them in Estrella, Uppercity or below, had the accuracy that Luxi possessed. It was not something she talked about.

The silence lay thick in the office.

Luxi swallowed hard. "I'm . . . I'm sorry, Gentle-fem Symposia."

Mercy sighed and folded her hands on her desktop. "I have been having strange dreams and odd . . . occurrences in my condo. I was led to believe that this man was an expert on such things." She gazed at her hands rather than at Luxi.

Luxi turned to get her purse hanging on her chair's slender arm. She pulled out a slim data card and set it on the desk. "This is a friend of mine. She'll take care of that for you, and she won't ask for more than she's worth. If you have any other problems, she'll tell you who you can trust."

Mercy took the card. She glanced briefly at it then tapped the edge on her desk. "When you told me, what you told me . . . I was under the impression that there was a lot more that you . . . didn't say."

Luxi closed her purse and nodded. With the entire company hard-wired for surveillance, 'embezzlement' was the one word that never came out of your mouth.

Mercy hands clenched into fists. "You just saved my career, didn't you?"

Luxi clutched her purse. "None of that will happen now. You're safe. He's not after you anymore." *He's after me.*

Mercy pressed her fingers to her brow and released a breath. "Damn it, Luxi, you just saved my ass, and I have to fire you!"

Luxi nodded miserably. She had done the right thing. She knew she'd done the right thing but, it still hurt like hell. "The company cannot afford to have me work in their offices." She closed her eyes. "I'm a . . . an information leak."

Mercy leaned back in her chair and glared at her closed office door. "It's also company policy to report strong talents. Once it's recorded on your personal essay, it goes on your resume. Not one company will hire you."

Luxi stared at her purse. "I know."

Mercy scowled at her hands. "You could have kept your mouth shut."

I would have lost my job anyway. Luxi lifted her shoulder in a half-hearted shrug. "I'm a nice girl. It's what nice girls do."

Mercy blinked then smiled bitterly. "Nice girls, huh?" She stared at her holographic display and tapped her desktop with a manicured nail. "Loyalty should be rewarded — not punished!" Abruptly, she leaned forward. "Luxi, can you look for yourself? Can you see if there is any way I can help you? Any way at all?"

Luxi's fingers tightened on her purse. Within her mind, her talent hummed, and possibilities dropped into place. This was it. She had reached the juxtaposition moment she'd been waiting for, the turning point in her personal future where everything came together and hinged on a single decision. She glanced up at her former supervisor. "As a matter of fact, there is."

CHAPTER ONE

Port Destiny Station
Imperial Space – Outbound Corridor

"We are approaching dock to *Port Destiny* spaceport," the shuttle's gentle voice announced. "Please secure all personal belongings in preparation for return to gravity."

Luxi woke from her nap and stretched in her padded chair. The shuttle trip had taken nearly an hour to cross the distance from the starliner to the spaceport. A zero-gravity nap had filled the time nicely.

She peered up over the heads of the other shuttle passengers. The yawning mouth of *Port Destiny's* sixty-five-meter wide docking bay door filled the forward view-screen. The cylindrical station slowly took on truly gigantic proportions. All of a sudden, Luxi had no trouble at all believing that the station employed over sixty-five hundred people

From the star liner's stateroom view-screens the station had appeared small. Measured against the spaceport station she had transferred from, *Port Destiny* station *was* small. It was only a little over eight kilometers long and archaic in design. Rather than a modern docking ring around a habitat globe, *Port Destiny* was an old Terran-built station that was tubular in shape. The entire barrel-like body of the station turned, generating nearly normal gravity the old-fashioned way, by centrifugal rotation.

Luxi pursed her lips. *Port Destiny* was practical rather than aesthetically pleasing, but practicality had its advantages.

8

Since the entire station turned, pocket regions of the station were less likely to lose gravity through unexpected power outages.

"Please remain in your seats until the shuttle has come to a complete stop," the shuttle's voice continued. "Please have your data cards ready for swift assessment through customs. Thank you for traveling with *Imperial Princess Star-lines*."

Luxi reached into the zip-sealed breast pocket of her deep violet jumpsuit and pulled out her holographic data card. The card marked her identity, such as it was, the last of her personal credits and her passage through the corridors of space on her way to a new planet, a new job and a new life. A reward from Ms. Symposia for her loyalty and the price she had paid for it.

The first moment she had touched the card, Luxi's talent for reading the future betrayed that her arrival at the card's final destination would mark the beginning of a long stable career marked by utter misery.

She was going to loathe her new life.

However, a crossing thread marking a single moment in time heavily weighted by chance, hinted that an opportunity for a better future could cross her path before she ever arrived. It was only a whisper among the tangled threads of synchronicity. A possible knot of juxtaposition whose threads were not yet in place. Others had yet to make decisions that would bring this moment of opportunity forth.

That slim possibility was enough to make Luxi sell every trace of her entire life. One hand-carry-bag and the card were all she had left.

Luxi bit her lip as the view-screen filled with the interior lights of the station's dock. She had traveled for sixteen days and eight jumps from star system to star system, on two different star-liners—to reach that moment. It was here, on Port Destiny station that the tangled threads of opportunity, chance, and decision would cross. It was here that her last chance for happiness would occur. Her talent hummed actively within her. Possibility was coming closer to being opportunity with every breath she took.

Luxi hoped with everything in her that the opportunity presented itself soon, because yet another moment of synchronicity was actively chasing her with malevolent determination.

The ghost-possessed monk, Vincent, was trailing her across the stars.

She could feel his vile intent crawling across the threads of possibility into her future. Her talent warned that no matter what course she charted, sooner or later he would catch up with her. From that meeting, all her lines into the future ended in a single moment marked by a single decision; a decision that was entirely in her own hands.

With not one hint of what that decision would bring — or cost.

Customs was a huge, well-lit, and crowded hallway that curved to the right. Three lines of passengers moved at a crawl past plain and featureless cream walls painted with a broad band of bronze. The long lines ended in a wide doorway blocked by full-body scanners and armed guards in dark uniforms. Their snug, half-armored doublet coats were emblazoned with: Sojourn Corp. across their breast and swords graced their hips. In the sealed environment of a space station, where a pinhole could mean the deaths of thousands, energy weapons were tightly controlled. Even the state of the art live-steel blade worn by Imperial Officers could not cut through armored plating.

Luxi tucked an errant wave of her red mane behind her ear. The shuttle's zero-g had really done a job on her hair. She was going to have to dig out her brush and re-braid the whole mess.

Boredom weighed heavily. It had been a long, dull flight, then a long, dull wait, and then this long, dull walk.

She arrived at the gate to enter the station proper and had to force herself not to yawn in the guard's face.

He winced. "Please don't yawn," he said softly. "I'll start doing it, then the rest of the guys will do it, and it looks really bad on surveillance."

Luxi smiled to cover the almost-yawn. "You? Yawn, when you have such an exciting job?" She turned over her data card for assessment.

"Oh, yeah . . ." He rolled his eyes and grinned. "I'm so fulfilled." He slid her card through his hand-held reader. The light over the doorway scanner went green. He returned her card and handed her a folded flyer emblazoned with the station's logo. "Welcome to *Port Destiny Station*." He leaned closer and added in a stage whisper, " . . . where nothing ever happens."

"Thank you." She glanced at the station flyer. "Personally, I've had enough adventure already."

The guard snorted. "Then you are going to love *Port Destiny*."

"I certainly hope so!" Luxi grinned and stepped through the scanner towing her overstuffed hand-carry-bag on its small wheels. No alarms went off. She released a small breath and continued on, grinning foolishly as she strode past another set of guards, and out of the customs ring. It was time to find her future.

The good news was that she didn't have to worry about getting on the next flight for a whole thirty hours, so she had thirty hours to figure out where she needed to be—and be there.

The bad news was that she didn't have the credits to get even a cheap room to rest in for any of those thirty hours. Her berths and meals were included on the star-liners, but the spaceport stopovers had proved very expensive. According to her personal account, she had just enough credits left to get a cup of kaffa and a snack. If she wanted a decent meal before her next flight, she was going to have to do something to make the credits to buy it. Luckily there wasn't a spaceport that didn't have a kaffa shop and a kaffa shop that didn't appreciate a good fortuneteller.

Letting the corporate office know that she could read the future could get her fired, but here in the middle of nowhere, it was a way to make a little cash.

Luxi held up the paper flyer the customs officer had handed her, reading as she walked. According to the flyer, there were seventeen kaffa shops in the station's Garden District Concourse. And according to her talent, she definitely had an appointment with one of them.

Luxi approached the row of lifts that would drop her on the Garden District Concourse. Her talent shifted within her.

Something didn't feel right.

She stopped, letting the other shuttle passengers brush by her. *Now what?* She frowned in concentration, trying to get a better grasp of what she was feeling.

Synchronicity was out of place. Taking the lift wouldn't put her in the right place in the right moment in time for the future she was chasing.

Luxi rolled her eyes in disgust. *Great, a complication . . .* Following the lines toward the future was proving to be a real pain in the ass. She glanced around. *Okay, so if I'm not supposed to go down the lift, where am I supposed to go?* There was a small hallway off to her right. Something clicked into place. *Ah . . .*

Following the thread of synchronicity, Luxi slipped through the line of passengers and into the small hallway.

The hall ended at a single lift access. According to the sign by the call button, this lift led to the cable-car tramway that traveled from one end of the station to the other, right through the station's center. No one was waiting on the lift.

Luxi's brow rose. Apparently, it was not a popular mode of transportation. But this was where she was supposed to be, so . . . She pushed the call button.

Chapter Two

Luxi stepped out on the tramway deck trailing her carry-bag and grabbed onto the rail that ran all the way around the tram station. Gravity was very minimal this close to the station's center.

Not one person was waiting on the tram.

On the other side of the deep track where the cable-tram would pull in, was a huge window, and beyond it, the floor of the world turned upward very slowly, meters and meters, and meters away — all the way overhead. *Oh Glory . . .*

She suddenly felt as though she were falling and falling and falling . . .

Luxi had to consciously make an effort not to fall over. According to her sense of perspective, the entire world was revolving sideways at a dizzying distance. She tore her gaze away and turned her back to the window. *Okay, let's not look at that anymore.* She swallowed, suddenly understanding why the tramway had few passengers.

According to the chrono on the wall between the two lifts, she had about five minutes to wait for the next tram. Once she was on it, the tram would reach a stop just short of every five minutes, and she had seven stops before she would reach the stop she wanted. *That should be long enough to do something about my hair.* Brushing her hair would also give her something to concentrate on, rather than the dizzying view. She knelt and dug into her bag to retrieve her brush.

Brush in hand, she stood to tug the elastic free from the end of her braid then dug her fingers into her thick mane to get it

14

out of the braid. It took more effort than she thought it would to untangle the long curls enough to pull a brush through it. The bright copper of her waist-length mane blazed in a cloud of sunset waves against her deep violet suit. She winced. Her hair was beyond frizzy. The shipboard sonic projection vibro-showers and antibacterial lighting had not been good for it. Brushing it in low gravity did not help any. She shook her head and kept brushing. Well at least her mane wasn't dry and crispy . . .

The lift door on her far left opened up, and three laughing people came leaping out of the lift, floating on the light gravity. The tallest was a pale young male with a sleek blonde mane of rich cream that swept well past his shoulders. His charcoal gray silk formal frockcoat flared open to his knees showing off the expanse of his gently defined bare chest. His trousers were skintight black velvet.

His two companions were slender black-haired fems dressed in snug and aggressive black leather trousers and tall boots. They were nearly masculine in build with only the gentle flare of hips and the slight curve of breasts under their cropped halter tops defining their gender. They were also armed with long and short blades, where the male was not. Their bare arms and bellies proudly displayed sword-cut scars across their light golden skin. Their mouths were wide, and their up-tilted black eyes flashed with humor as they towed their beautiful companion toward the tram-track.

Luxi watched them avidly as she pulled her brush through her long mane. From the looks of the sword scars, the fems were a lot older than their youthful forms. It was entirely possible that the male was also far older than he appeared. Clearly, she was looking at an Imperial Lord and his two bodyguards.

The young male turned to look at Luxi with violet eyes set in an exquisitely perfect face. His glossed pink lips opened on a spectacular smile.

Luxi froze. *Wow . . . pretty.*

Another man came out of the lift. His strongly masculine face was pale as marble, without a trace of blush. His metallic-silver mane was drawn back and fastened in a smooth straight tail that fell just past his shoulders. His full-body, high-collared jumpsuit was of deepest black, yet it shimmered with rainbows. Absolutely comfortable in the light gravity, he moved with the inhumanly effortless grace of the mechanically enhanced. He was simply gorgeous in motion. He stalked around the incredible trio with the careful inattention of a predator trying not to startle his prey.

Luxi blinked. There was something odd about him . . . His hair was true metallic-silver, a color no living hair could possibly emulate. Her mouth fell open. He was a cyborg—the most perfectly crafted, utterly human-looking cyborg she had ever seen.

He lifted his chin as though scenting something interesting and turned to look at Luxi with eyes the color of steel—and shadow.

Luxi's talent jolted hard. *Good Glory . . .*

The cyborg was animate and conscious, but he wasn't alive. The spirit of the living man he had once been burned in the depths of his gaze, a spirit that had not fled with the loss of his living body; a ghost perfectly contained in fully robotic flesh.

Within her, synchronicity suddenly dropped into place.

The cyborg was a key to the future she was looking for.

Luxi jerked her gaze away from the stunning ghost. *A haunted cyborg?* Life was getting stranger by the second. She lifted the brush to her hair, to do something rather than turn back to stare at him. Her talent for sensing synchronicity shimmered within her. Apparently, she was supposed to see him, and he was supposed to see her, so he had something to do with her new future, but what?

She scowled, trying to read the lines, but just could not see what was supposed to happen next. The future was still too vague. Apparently, the decision to set things in motion was not hers . . .

Someone spoke at her elbow.

"Huh?" Luxi turned.

The beautiful young lord and his two dark-eyed companions stood only inches away. Luxi's eyes opened wide. This close, the young lord was breathtaking. His face had only the slightest touches of cosmetics outlining his impossibly violet eyes. Even his perfume was gorgeous.

He asked her a question.

She had no clue what he said. Luxi bit her lip and lifted her shoulder in a small shrug. "I'm sorry, but I don't understand?" She really, really needed to get an upgrade for her internal translator.

"He says that you have hair like living flame. He'd like to know if you would care to join him for sex."

Luxi started and turned her head to find the cyborg standing by her left elbow. She hadn't even seen him approach. She was forced to look up. He was head and shoulders taller than she was, and this close, he was absolutely stunning. The lord was lovely, but the cyborg's arresting face was utterly, powerfully masculine. Something in her stilled, as though holding its breath.

His dark silver brows rose. "Are you all right?"

Luxi released her breath and felt her cheeks heat. She'd been staring. "Sorry . . . I . . . ." What had she been thinking? She didn't have a clue. Her mind had utterly blanked. "I don't know your name?"

"I'm Leto." He smiled.

"I'm Luxi." Her voice came out breathless. Glory above, his smile! She felt the listening stillness wash through her again.

Leto tilted his head toward the lord and his two fems. "He's waiting to know if you want to have sex."

Luxi blinked alert. "He wants . . . what?"

Leto lifted a pale hand to cover his chuckle. "Sex. He wants to know if you want to have sex with him and his fems."

Luxi glanced over at the beautiful lord then bit her lip. "Could you tell him, I'm flattered, but I don't normally have . . ." She winced. "Relations, with people I don't know?"

Leto lifted his chin and replied to the lord.

The lord rolled his eyes in obvious amusement. His two companions dissolved into giggles. The lord glanced at the cyborg and asked a question.

Leto raised his chin and turned away.

The lord watched Luxi expectantly and smiled.

Luxi peered up at the cyborg. "Leto, what did he say?"

Leto folded his arms across his chest and glanced down at the deck. "Tell you what; I'll translate what he said for the price of . . ." He turned to Luxi and lifted a silver brow. "A kiss."

"A kiss?" Luxi's breath caught. This spectacular man wanted to kiss *her*?

His shadow-filled eyes focused on her. "Will you kiss me?"

Glory yes! Luxi licked her lips. "Okay."

Leto's eyes widened just a hair. He leaned downward, very slowly.

Luxi tilted her chin up to meet him. His lips brushed hers. Warmth, breath . . . He was warm, he breathed. Her eyes drifted closed, and her lips parted under his. Their tongues met, explored, parried. He tasted like fresh, clean water. He smelled of rich leather.

He cupped her shoulders in his strong hands.

She reached for him, and her hands settled on his hips. His shimmering suit was warm under her palms and felt like exotic leather. Vibrancy and darkness pulsed in a delicious yet

18

shivery combination under her fingertips. She spread her fingers and pressed her palms against him to feel more of it.

His hands slid up her neck, drawing tiny shivers, and his fingers slid under her mane. He cupped her head and angled her mouth to deepen the kiss, stroking her tongue, tasting her, encouraging her to kiss him back.

Heat, hunger, urgency . . . A small moan escaped her throat. Her hands slid around his waist, pulling him closer.

His arm closed around her waist, pulling her tight against his body.

He was warm and excited. She could feel the hard length of his erection against her belly. Moisture dampened her panties. The simmering dark within him brushed against her heart with unexpected fire. Her talent awoke in a searing rush, and suddenly she could feel his bare skin under her palms and along her entire body where they touched.

Leto abruptly pulled away, blinking, clearly startled.

Luxi grabbed onto his belt, refusing to let him go. "Did I do something wrong?"

He frowned down at her. "I 'felt' you." He licked his lips. "You're vitae sensitive? You can feel life forces?"

"Not exactly . . ." She blushed. There was just no way to say this gracefully. "I feel . . . ghosts. I'm necro-sensitive."

"I see." Leto's brows lowered, and his eyes narrowed. "Did you know that I was . . ." He took a breath, and his jaw tightened. "*Dead*, before you kissed me?"

She nibbled on her bottom lip. "I knew that you were a cyborg with a . . . ghost."

He stilled, then his eyes narrowed. "And you kissed me anyway?"

She frowned up at him. "Is there a reason I shouldn't?"

He blinked and gave her a sour smile. "About a million of them; all religious and having to do with necrophilia."

She raised a sarcastic brow. "Funny, you don't kiss like a

corpse. You're warm, you breathe."

He barked out a laugh and stared downward. "I didn't think so either, but some people seem to have a problem with it." He shook his head and folded his hands slid behind him. "I was originally a nano-based cyborg. Biological machines replaced my body cell by cell. I'm not living tissue anymore, but I'm still me and perfectly functional; just not biological, so to speak."

Luxi snorted and glanced down at the heavy line of his erection straining against the seam of his suit. "You felt awfully biological to me." Her fingers tightened on his belt. She had the most incredible urge to pull him close and 'touch' him again.

Trilling laughter reminded Luxi sharply that they were not alone. She turned to face the grinning lord and his dark-eyed and aggressive companions.

The lord gestured and shot out a rapid-fire list of incomprehensible statements at Leto and glanced at Luxi briefly. He watched the cyborg expectantly.

A windy roar announced the sudden arrival of the tram.

Leto nodded at the lord

The lord grinned then turned to his two fems, and they all moved toward the tram through the tram station's low gravity like swimmers through water.

Leto tilted his head at Luxi. "Is that your bag?"

Luxi frowned at the tram. It was going in the wrong direction. "Yes, but that's not my tram."

Leto snatched for the handle of her bag and caught her around the waist. "It is now." He jumped.

CHAPTER THREE

Luxi grabbed onto Leto's arm as their feet left the deck in a spectacular leap boosted by the weak gravity. She gasped as Leto carried her clear across to the tram's open door.

"In you go!" He shoved her onto the tram, right behind the youthful trio.

Just outside the tram's outward facing windows the floor of world turned upward very slowly, meters and meters, and meters away.

Luxi gasped and turned away from the rolling view. Her sense of perspective and balance simply could not deal with it. The tram was windowed on both sides with long cushioned benches running lengthwise under the windows. Once the tram left the small station, the world would revolve all the way around with the tram moving through the very center. It was going to be impossible to avoid the stomach-churning view.

Leto was the only thing to look at besides the floor. He was also the only thing to hold on to. She grabbed his belt. "Leto, what are you doing?"

Leto grinned at her and turned her to face the tram's interior. "We are going to provide them with some entertainment." He pushed her deeper into the tram, aiming for the cushioned bench along the left.

On the opposite side, the pale lord stretched his arms out across the back of the bench, relaxing as his fems stripped off their weapons with astonishing speed. He smiled and licked his lips, staring hard at Luxi and the cyborg pushing her down the aisle.

The two fems climbed up on the bench and knelt on either side of the pale lord, framing him. They glanced at each other and licked their lips, then leaned close to pull his coat open, baring his pale chest. They pressed and rubbed their lithe golden bodies against his creamy skin, spreading their slender fingers wide to caress his gently defined chest and smooth belly.

He groaned and shifted under them, rubbing up against them.

They pushed his creamy mane back from his neck, and pink tongues flashed as they licked his throat.

He raised his chin and tipped his head back with an open-mouthed sigh, but kept his violet gaze locked on Luxi and the cyborg.

Leto's lips brushed her ear. "Just so you know, the blond is Bel, the fem on his right is Orah, and the fem on his left is Faro."

Luxi tried to stop, but Leto was impossible to halt. The light gravity gave her feet no purchase whatsoever on the floor. "Leto, I am *not* going to have sex with them!"

"No, *they* are going to have sex." He shoved her bag under the bench "But they want to do it while watching us kiss." He caught her around the waist and dropped onto the broad seat, tugging her down across his lap.

Luxi's butt landed on the seat between Leto's thighs. She grabbed for his shoulders. "Wait a minute; they're having sex on the tramway?"

Leto shook his head and cradled her in his arms. "Haven't you ever had sex on a tramway before?"

Luxi shifted on his lap. "No! And I'm not having it now!"

Leto tightened his hold, settling her across his thighs. "Relax. *They* are having sex. *We* are just kissing."

Orah caught a fist full of her lord's silky mane at the base of his neck, opened her mouth wide on his throat, and bit down on the long muscle.

He gasped and smiled.

Faro licked her way down Bel's throat to his pale pink nipple and stroked it with an outstretched tongue. She locked her lips around the pale flesh and sucked, her mouth making wet sounds as she moaned her delight.

Bel writhed, and a soft moan escaped. He wrapped his arm around Faro and pulled her tighter against his chest. He reached out and wrapped his arm around Orah as she bit down on his neck. He whispered to them, but his gaze remained on Luxi and Leto.

Orah released her lord's throat from her teeth and leaned back to pull her top off, revealing the gentle curves of her breasts and her tightly pointed caramel nipples.

Bel pulled her tight against him and turned his head to capture her proud nipple in his mouth, but his eyes never left Luxi and Leto. His tongue flashed as he licked first one nipple then the other, then his teeth as he bit down.

Orah arched, throwing her head back and moaning, tugging his hair to encourage him.

Bel reached up to catch Faro's cropped black hair in his fist and pushed her head from his nipple down toward his lap.

Faro spilled across Bel's lap and stretched out on the bench, kicking her feet up. She tugged Bel's belt open and unfastened his pants. Her hand slipped within. Her fingers were plainly defined by the elastic velvet of his trousers as she wrapped her hand around his cock and then pushed deeper to cup his balls.

Bel gasped and arched, bringing his hips up from the bench.

Luxi swallowed as wet heat pulsed in her core from the inciting view. "Just kissing?"

Leto's breath caressed her ear. "I swear I will not go any

further than you want to go."

Luxi shivered and bit her lip. *That's what I'm afraid of.* She was already more excited than she had ever been with anyone else. Her talent hummed within her. She was still in the right place, occupying the right moment in time. She was supposed to be here, doing this. "Okay . . ."

Leto gave her a heart-stopping if sly smile. "Good." He leaned closer and took her mouth, pressing her back against his arm as the tram began to move through the heart of the turning station.

Leto's taste, clean and fresh, his scent, tinged with leather, and the determined pursuit of his tongue against hers combined into a drugging euphoria that cleared Luxi's mind of thought while crowding her body with restless yearning.

His mouth encouraged her to arch further back. "Look," he whispered. "Look at them."

Luxi turned to look at the pale lord and his fems across the aisle.

Faro, sprawled across Bel's lap, grinned as she pulled his cock free of his trousers. The pale column of his hardening length curved upward from the black velvet, fully two of her hand-widths in length. She tightened her fingers around him and stroked upward, then down. The deep rose cockhead darkened to plum. She stretched out her tongue and licked the column of pale flesh in her hand. Her tongue lashed the flared edge of his darkening cockhead.

Bel's eyes closed briefly, and he released Orah's nipple to gasp out a short phrase.

Orah pulled back from Bel's arm to stand up on the bench, her nipples wet from his mouth. She grabbed the overhead safety bar with one hand and jerked her leather pants down with her other. Her pants slid past her hips, baring the muscular curve of her ass and her neatly trimmed black mons.

Leto fingers tugged at the throat fastenings of Luxi's suit.

Slowly, carefully, he opened her suit to her heart. His hot wet mouth closed on her throat, and he licked. His teeth raked the long muscle and over her pulse.

Luxi shivered and her mouth opened on a gasp, but she kept her eyes on the pale young lord and his two fems.

Bel wrapped his arm around Orah's hips and pulled her toward his mouth. He stretched out his tongue and licked the plump lips of her exposed pussy. He tightened his hold and thrust his tongue deeper, licking with audible wet enthusiasm.

Orah whimpered, her hips rolling against his mouth and lifted her booted foot to step over his lap.

Bel released Faro's hair and shoved the nearly naked Orah back to his side. He clearly did not want his view of Luxi and Leto blocked.

Faro, in his lap, opened her mouth and took the plum head within. Her lips tightened around Bel's cock, and her head plunged, taking him deep in her mouth, and into her throat. Her head rose and fell, her cheeks hollowing as she sucked with wet enthusiasm.

Leto slid his hand down Luxi's suited hip. He cupped then caressed her butt cheek.

Shivers trailed across her skin, followed by sudden heat. Luxi shifted against him releasing a small moan. She could feel his palm as though he stroked her bare skin. It was his ghost. She was feeling the phantom within his cybernetic hand touching her, right through her clothes.

"Blood and Fate, I can feel you," Leto whispered against Luxi's throat. "I've never felt anyone with my . . ." He hesitated for a breath. "That part of me, before."

"Your spirit?" Luxi flashed him a quick smile.

He bit his lip. "Yeah, my spirit, sure."

"Can you feel me?" She leaned back to press her palm to his heart.

"Here." He moved her hand over to the right and a little lower on his chest. He closed his eyes and drew in a breath. "Oh yeah, right on the nipple."

Luxi shifted her fingers. She could actually feel the hard nub right through his suit. She could feel his leather suit, too, but the suit didn't seem to feel quite as real as the tight nipple under her fingers. She rubbed her thumb across it.

He pressed her palm tight, stilling her hand. "It feels as though you're touching my bare nipple, but deeper."

Luxi peered up at him. "That's what it feels like to me."

His brows shot up. "Really? How about this?" His fingers slid across her hip and over her belly, tracing very lightly over her suit.

She shivered. It was the most incredibly exciting thing she'd ever felt. "It's like . . . I'm naked."

His eyes narrowed and his lips curved up in a sly smile. "Is that so?"

Her pulse suddenly beat in her throat. Perhaps that had not been a good thing to say. "Wait . . ."

"Oh no, you can't take it back now!" He pressed her back onto the bench pinning her shoulders with his hands. Her long red mane spilled over the seat and onto the floor.

"Leto!" She shoved her hands up against his chest. "What are you doing?"

He licked his lips and chuckled softly. "What do you think?" He came up on one knee and threw his leg over her hips, dropping a booted foot to the floor to straddle her. "I want to see just how naked you feel!"

"Leto please!" She could barely speak past the pulse in her throat. She desperately wanted to feel his skin against hers. The thought of it was seriously soaking her panties. She didn't think she'd ever wanted to feel anyone more. But if he actually did it, she didn't think he would stop there. Worse, she didn't think she would want him to stop there.

"Luxi . . ." He lowered his mouth and his lips brushed hers.

She moaned and opened to receive his kiss.

He turned his head to take her mouth more fully, his tongue making deep slow sweeps as he slowly dropped to his elbows. His chest brushed her breasts. His warm skin swept across her hardened nipples as though nothing lay between them.

She couldn't stop her moan any more than she could stop herself from arching to press her breasts more fully against him.

His hand slid between the seat's back and her hip to cup her thigh. He pulled and her knee rose. He set his knee on the seat between her thighs and shifted his weight onto the seat. His other hand pushed her leg from the seat to get both his knees up on the seat.

And between her thighs.

Alarm washed through Luxi. *Glory and mercy!* Fully dressed, this was a perfectly harmless position, but for some reason, their clothes weren't any kind of a barrier between them.

She jerked her mouth from his, but he pursued her, capturing her lips and then her hands, pulling them up over her head. Stretched out and spread, she moaned into his mouth.

He lowered his hips against hers, groaned and arched.

Luxi sucked in a sharp breath. She could feel him. Feel his skin sliding against her skin, and his rigid cock rubbing with intimate warmth against her belly.

He released her hands and slid his arms under and around her shoulders, pulling her tight against him. "Blood and hell, you feel damned good!"

She groaned in reply. He felt damned good, too. The urge to feel more of him brought her arms up to press her hands against his back. She could feel the ridges of his muscular form under her palms. He was fully dressed, but he felt utterly and excitingly naked.

CHAPTER FOUR

Bel grinned at Luxi and Leto as he lapped at Orah's pussy while his hips bucked into Faro's mouth. He turned to look down at the sucking fem and snapped out a phrase before returning his mouth to Orah trembling in his hold.

Her mouth full of Bel's cock, Faro unfastened her pants.

Bel slid his palm down Faro's spine and shoved his hand into the back of her loosened leather trousers. Her snug pants defined his fingers as he cupped and fondled her ass. He groaned and shoved his hand deeper, his fingers curving under and between her cheeks.

Faro whimpered as she sucked, lifting her hips and pumping her ass against his hand.

"Are you watching them?" Leto whispered in Luxi's ear. His hands slid down to cup her ass, pressing her more firmly against his cock.

"Yes." Luxi had been unable to tear her eyes off them, even with the heat of Leto's body rubbing against her belly and breasts.

"Bel has his fingers shoved in Faro's ass."

Luxi's eyes widened. "He does not!"

Leto chuckled and his hands tightened on her ass cheeks. "Trust me, I know what I'm looking at, and he is finger-fucking her ass hard."

Luxi frowned and shifted under him. "And she likes it?"

"Are you joking?" He lifted his chin toward the lascivious view. "She's about to cum." He lifted his head and hissed a soft phrase at the sucking fem.

Faro's gaze turned to Leto, releasing the hard cock in her mouth. Her eyes widened. She gasped and trembled, pumping hard against Bel's hand with her eyes locked on Leto. A soft moan escaped, and she froze. Her eyes dilated wide and she shuddered hard. Her eyes drifted closed and she writhed with a smile on her lips.

Leto sighed. "There. She came."

Orah, locked to Bel's mouth whimpered desperately and grabbed onto his head with both hands, grinding against his mouth.

Leto nodded. "The other one is about to cum."

Bel pulled his mouth away, drawing moans of disappointment from Orah.

Leto chuckled. "Oh, that was mean. He didn't let her cum."

Bel grinned and tugged on Orah's knees.

Orah fell back onto the bench with a soft gasp.

Bel snapped out a phrase.

Orah flipped over onto her belly, coming up on her elbows and knees. She put one booted foot down on the tram's floor, spreading herself wide.

Leto sighed. "Ah, that's why. They're going to fuck."

Bel turned to face Orah and came up on his knee. He grabbed her by the hips and pulled her toward his jutting cock. He jerked her pants lower and turned to look over his shoulder.

Faro grabbed her top and yanked it over her head, showing the even slighter curves of her breasts and her stiff caramel nipples. She tossed the top on the seat behind her and came up on her knees behind Bel. She tugged at the waistband of her open pants, tugging them lower. A small but not inconsiderable cock emerged as she pulled her pants down past her hips.

Luxi stiffed in surprise. "She's a boy?"

Leto snorted. "No, the little he-fem is both. Faro is fully

equipped with both sexes, but her body looks female, so she's still considered a fem."

"Then she has a . . ." Luxi swallowed. "She has a pussy too?"

"Oh yes."

Luxi frowned up at him. "How do you know all this?"

Leto smiled. "Who do you think Bel invited for sex first? He was quite vocal about his little he-fem's talents."

"You were going to have sex with them?"

"Ah, no." Leto gave her a tight smile. "That young man has a dominant streak a mile wide. I wasn't interested in playing his games, but I was more than interested in watching, so I followed them up." He brushed his lips against Luxi's ear. "Bel likes to be watched almost as much as he likes fucking people he doesn't know."

Luxi whispered back. "That's really perverted."

"No, it's boredom." Leto grinned. "And you seem to be finding it rather entertaining."

Luxi ground her teeth. "Fine, rub it in."

Leto licked his lips. "Don't mind if I do."

Bel positioned himself behind Orah and gripped his cock. He grabbed her thigh and pulled her back onto him. His head came up and he groaned as his shaft slowly disappeared into the trembling fem's dripping cunt. He stopped, caught both her thighs and pulled back to suddenly thrust deep into her.

Orah shoved back against him, meeting his strong thrust.

Behind them, Faro stroked her small cock to hardness and tugged Bel's velvet trousers down past his hips.

"Oh yeah, all three are going to fuck. Good genetic designing, the he-fem rearmed fast, though I don't envy the mess in his trousers."

Luxi blinked. "What?"

"Faro already came, remember? There's a load of cum in her pants." He made a sour face. "Not something you want to walk around in."

Luxi bit her lip in. Wet panties weren't exactly comfortable either. "Why did he let Faro cum, but not Orah?"

Leto grinned. "To keep the little he-fem from cumming too fast once she got her dick up his tight ass."

Faro locked one arm around Bel's hips and positioned her cock between his cheeks.

Bel stilled, waiting.

Faro arched her hips, pushing her cock into Bel's ass. She sighed and grinned then locked both arms around his hips.

Bel groaned and licked his pale pink lips. A grin appeared. He gripped Orah's thighs and ground his cock deep into her, then pulled back, pressing himself back onto Faro's cock. He thrust, and pulled back, then thrust, fucking and being fucked, with slow deep plunges and retreats.

Both fems gasped and moaned in obvious enjoyment.

"Speaking of cumming . . ." Leto reached for the fastening at Luxi's heart and tugged her jumpsuit further open.

Luxi sucked in a breath, as cool air caressed her flushed skin. The suit was designed to be opened for necessities, without having to take it off. It unfastened all the way to down and up over her butt.

Leto's mouth captured hers as his fingers worked, unfastening her suit lower and lower . . .

She didn't try to stop him. She didn't have the will to stop him. She moaned into his mouth. The absolute truth was; she didn't want him to stop.

He released her suit fastening all the way down and then under, as far as it would go. He grabbed the edges and pulled her suit apart, exposing her flushed nipples, her belly, and her panties. His brows shot up. "Panties?"

Luxi bit her lip and flushed. "Well, of course."

Leto grinned. "How sweet!"

Bel, across from them, rolled his eyes and chuckled as he

continued to slow-fuck his two writhing and anxious fems. He reached under to cup Orah's breasts and tugged on her hard little nipples.

Leto leaned down and captured Luxi's nipple with his lips and his teeth.

Fire scorched from her nipple straight down to her clit, drawing an echoing throb. Luxi gasped and arched. A spat of cream released into her panties.

His hand slid into her panties, his long fingers delving past the plump outer lips of her sex to explore her intimate folds. "You're wet." He stroked her clit lightly and insistently.

Luxi threw back her head and moaned, jolted by the bolts of erotic fire caused by his deft touch on her clit. He was really, really good. She had to fight to keep a coherent thought in her head. "I thought we weren't going to do sex?"

"Do you want me to stop?" He stroked her hard nipple with his pointed tongue while strumming her swollen clit with devastating skill.

Luxi writhed and gasped. She could barely think past the fire boiling and building in her core, but she knew for a fact she was well past the stopping point.

"Luxi," he whispered and swept his tongue across her painfully swollen nipples. He slid a finger into her core and stroked. "Do you want me to stop?"

Luxi shivered and arched her hips up against him, deliberately rubbing against his cock. "No."

"Good." Leaving his hand in her panties, he leaned over against the backrest and grabbed the fastenings to his suit with his other hand. He jerked the clips open from his throat all the way down to where the rigid line of his cock began, then dropped back over her. He focused on her with eyes filled with heat, and shadow. "Touch me."

Luxi reached up and swept her palms across the smooth skin of his chest then ran her fingers down his belly. She could feel his other body, his phantom, his ghost, pulsing right under the smoothness of his cybernetic skin. "Oh . . ."

"Blood and Fate, that feels good." He moaned. "Lower. Touch my cock."

His cock? Luxi hesitated.

Leto groaned and his steel eyes burned with shadows. "If I can't fuck you, at least give me your hand."

Luxi bit her lip. He had a point. His hand was already in her pants. It was only fair. And she wanted to. She really, really wanted to feel his cock. She slid her hand down his muscular belly and into his suit. Her fingers brushed against the thick root of his cock. She opened her hand and reached deeper, wrapping her fingers around him. His skin was hot and smooth. She explored his length. He was long and very thick.

Leto threw his head back and gasped. "Bloody, fucking Fate! That is fucking intense! It's like I have two and you're holding them both."

Curious, Luxi pulled him free of his suit. His cock was bone white, hot, and marble hard in her fingers. Leto was a big man. She stroked him, pulling upward toward the flared head, then slid her thumb across the broad head.

"Oh, shit!" He shuddered and arched back with a gasp, pulling away from her hand. "I can't take it. It's too much." He winced as he tucked himself back into his suit. "I'm going to have to settle for rubbing against you." He flashed a broad grin then dropped down on top her. "You don't mind, do you?"

Luxi grinned. "I don't know; I kind of liked the idea of having you go to pieces in my hand."

Leto snorted. "You would." He slid his hands down her body, caught her thighs, and lifted. "Let's see if I can return the favor." His mouth took her nipple and bit down.

Luxi shivered under his teeth then felt his cock nudge and

rub against the intimate folds of her body's entrance. She stiffened. "Leto?"

He licked her nipple. "Relax, my dick is still in my pants." He leaned over to take the other nipple into his teeth.

Fate and Glory he was good with his mouth! Luxi moaned. "Then what am I feeling?"

Leto lifted his head and grinned. "My . . . ah . . . spirit."

Luxi's mouth opened. His *spirit*?

"I can actually feel how wet you are. I wonder . . ." He thrust, entering her in one strong lunge, and gasped.

Luxi gasped with him. Regardless of the fact that his *spirit* was in her, rather than the hard cock she'd held, her body was quite convinced that a very hard cock was stretching her, and she hadn't had sex in quite a while. She shifted under him and felt the cock trapped in his suit riding right on her clit. She groaned, and her body abruptly moistened, easing the tightness within her.

"That is so strange. I can feel my dick in you, but I can also feel my dick in my pants."

Luxi swallowed. "You're telling me it's strange?"

He shifted his hips and hissed. "Blood and damnation, you feel good." He pulled back and thrust.

Luxi rolled under him, feeling his hard stroke and yet feeling his rigid cock against her clit too. Heat coiled tight and hard. She wrapped her legs around his hips purely out of carnal greed. It didn't matter that it wasn't his cock, whatever was in her felt damned good there.

"Damn . . ." Leto curled his arms under hers and grabbed her shoulders. "I can't tell the difference." He pulled and thrust and thrust . . ."It feels like I'm fucking you."

"Great," Luxi panted and writhed under him. "Because I sure feel like I'm being fucked!" His strokes were hitting something inside, and his cock was pressing hard on her clit, jolting her hard and fast toward a powerful climax. Her body shuddered and trembled around him.

Leto panted against her throat. "It feels like you're close to cumming too."

Luxi gasped. "Fastest one I've ever had."

"Good." He slowed down to long delicious strokes and withdraws. "But I don't want you to cum yet."

Luxi moaned and ground up against him. "Leto, please?"

"Oh, I like the sound of you begging, but no."

"No?" She twisted her hips.

"No." Leto grabbed her hips to still her. He turned to look at the three writhing on the opposite bench and his mouth set in a hard line.

Bel stared hard at Leto and Luxi, moving exquisitely slow. His fems were panting and writhing in erotic agony, right on the edge of a climax he wouldn't let them have.

Leto nodded at him.

Bel grabbed Orah by the hips and began thrusting ruthlessly hard into her with merciless speed.

Faro, behind him, matched him stroke for stroke, gasping with her thrusts.

All three turned to watch Leto.

Leto held Luxi still under him, thrusting just slowly enough to keep her on the edge and drive her insane. His gaze held, locked on the three moaning across the aisle.

Orah abruptly held her breath and shuddered. Her eyes widened as she stared at Leto, and her breath exploded with a mewling cry.

Abruptly Faro threw back her head and cried out.

Bel grinned and gasped, grabbing tight onto Orah as he thrust and held. His body trembled, and he thrust again, releasing a small shout followed by groaning gasps.

Luxi was suddenly aware of power sliding across her skin. It was centered on Leto. Her lesser talent stirred, the part of her that saw phantoms. A cloud of swirling colorless energy, like heat rising from hot metal, was surrounding him.

Something dark and hungry opened and bloomed within Leto's heart. He drew in a deep breath. The swirling energy dove into him, drawn into his body, and he drank it down, absorbing, and feeding the core of his shadowy heart.

Luxi's mouth fell open. Leto was feeding his ghost on the energy given off by their orgasm.

Leto sighed with deep appreciation. "Yes . . ." He smiled down at Luxi with the echo of his feeding burning in the heart of his eyes. "Now it's your turn to cum."

CHAPTER FIVE

Leto pulled Luxi up and sat back against the bench with her straddling his lap. He grinned. "Ready to fuck?"

Luxi grabbed onto his shoulders and moaned as the phantom cock within her shifted. She wasn't sure she wanted to feed his ghost with her orgasm, but her body didn't seem to care. It was tight with erotic tension, and it wanted release. She glanced over at the exhausted trio.

Bel and his fems were cuddled in half-naked, sweaty splendor, gently kissing and cuddling in his lap.

Luxi bit her lip. They didn't look at all like they had been harmed . . .

"Luxi . . ."

She turned to Leto only to have her mouth captured in a searing and aggressive kiss. His arms closed tight around her, and he pulled her hard against him, bare chest to bare breast.

She shivered and kissed him back. *Fuck it. They weren't hurt. I'll be fine.* She moaned softly and grabbed the shoulders of his suit. Damnit, she wanted to cum!

He thrust up into her and moaned into her mouth. He thrust again, then again . . .

Luxi closed her eyes tight and whimpered in reply. Sitting this way, his cock went deep, and he was big and hard, and delicious . . . Heat pooled, rose and boiled in her core.

Leto groaned and slid his hand down to cup her ass, lifting her then pushing her down onto his strokes.

She moaned and rocked against him. His cock, phantom or not, struck something electric within her that jolted her

38

toward orgasm with every hard thrust.

Abruptly, he locked his arm around her to hold her still. He tipped her back, and his mouth took her nipple. He bit down on the tender peak then licked away the sting. His hand moved between them, jerking at his suit.

Luxi arched and gasped as his mouth tenderly tortured her nipple.

Leto suddenly lifted her off his cock, repositioned and shoved back into her wet core. He threw his head back and shuddered. "Fuck!"

Luxi's breath exploded from her lungs. His physical cock was in her. She could feel them both simultaneously filling her. "Leto!"

He groaned and thrust, and thrust . . ."I'm already . . . fucking you." His panting breaths cut into his speech. "I'd rather . . . cum . . . in a nice warm . . . body . . . instead of . . . my pants." He ground up into her. "God, you feel good." He lifted her against his chest and began to power thrust hard.

Luxi writhed on the incredible sensation of fullness as he hammered up into her more than willing body. "You said . . . you . . . wouldn't!"

He bared his teeth, his jaw tight as he thrust. "Sometimes . . . I lie." He gasped. "You obviously like it. You're dripping . . . down my balls."

Luxi could only hold on as she was thoroughly and mercilessly fucked. "You're . . . a beast!"

"Sometimes." He leaned closer to nibble on her throat. "Shouldn't you be . . . screaming and trying to . . . escape?"

She shivered under his lips and tilted her head back to give his mouth better access. "Do you want me to?"

His hands closed tight on her ass. "I'd prefer if you didn't."

Luxi groaned and twisted. "Would you stop?"

"Nope." He shuddered and thrust faster. "Too close . . . to cumming . . . to stop."

Luxi bit back her building shriek. "Me, too."

"That's my girl!" Leto grinned. "You're about to cum."

"Yes," she whimpered. "Glory *yes*!"

Leto covered her mouth with his, stealing her breath in a ruthless kiss.

Tension broke within her and pleasure exploded in waves of lightning that rampaged through her leaving violent tremors in its wake. Luxi gasped her frantic cries into Leto's mouth and bucked hard.

His gaze caught hers — and pulled.

Within her heart, something broke free and found a place in his hungry soul. And she didn't care.

She collapsed against his shoulder, panting with repletion. She had never come harder in her life.

Leto held her, his hand sweeping down her spine. "That was phenomenal."

She smiled into his shoulder. "I bet you say that to everybody."

"No, I don't."

"Good." Luxi moaned and lifted to pull away. "Time to get up."

"Not just yet." Leto locked his arms around her hips, holding her tight onto him. "I'm still ejaculating."

Luxi leaned back to look at his face. "What? But, you're a cyborg!"

Leto smiled tiredly. "I was once completely biological. The nanotech just replaced what was already there." He rolled his hips under her and groaned. "So, I still cum. Thank Fate!"

Luxi sucked in a breath. She could feel him pulsing within her. "But you're not biological, so what are you putting in me?"

Leto pursed his lips. "Not quite sure."

Luxi raised her brow. "You don't know?"

He rolled his eyes at her. "The composition of my ejaculate

is not something I bothered to have examined." He groaned and lowered his arms, releasing her. "Okay, now my balls are empty."

"Gee, thanks." Luxi rose up and lifted her leg over him, dismounting to stand on trembling legs in the aisle. A clear, viscous liquid slithered down her thighs.

Grinning broadly, Faro held out a moist towelette.

Luxi shot Leto a sour look as she used the towelette to clean up the mess.

He grinned. "We definitely have to do this again sometime soon."

Luxi started fastening her suit, her eyes tight on her fingers rather than the view out the window or the smug cyborg. "We weren't supposed to do it in the first place, remember?"

Leto rose from the bench to fasten his suit. "Oh, come on, you enjoyed the hell out of it!"

Luxi winced in guilt. He was right. She hadn't done a whole lot to put a stop to it. In fact, she had been very willing at the end. She sighed. "Look, it doesn't matter, I can't see you again." A stab of regret shot through her.

His mouth tightened. "Why not?"

Luxi shook her head. "I'm only here on layover. I leave in less than thirty hours." To go to a job she was going to loathe.

Leto folded his arms stiffly across his chest. "Don't you want to see me again?" His jaw tightened.

Luxi bit back a smile. He seemed so disappointed. "What? So you can trick me into sex again?"

He gave her a tight smile. "Well, yeah."

She shook her head. "One track mind; and it's all in the commode."

He raised a brow and gave her a feral grin. "I'm male. Sue me."

The tram suddenly pulled into a station and halted.

Bel and his fems rose from the bench, once again fully

dressed and fully armed. They strode up the aisle toward the exit.

Luxi lifted her head. The tram was supposed to stop every five minutes, but it hadn't. Now that they had . . . finished, it stopped. She frowned. "Why didn't the tram stop before?"

Leto lifted his chin toward the exit. "His Imperial lordship didn't want the tram to halt, so it didn't. He has the access codes in his array." He tapped a finger against his brow.

Luxi's mouth fell open. "Bel really is a lord?" She reached down to collect her hand-bag from under the bench.

"You didn't know?"

"I wasn't sure. I've never seen an Imperial Lord before." She frowned. "He looked really young."

"That's because he had really good genetic engineering." Leto grinned. "He's about twice your age."

She frowned. "You never did tell me what he said, from before."

Leto lifted his chin and bit back a smile. "He saw the way you were watching me and asked me . . ." He took a breath and released it. "If I thought I could seduce you."

Luxi stilled. "And then we kissed."

Leto's brow lifted. "And then *you* kissed *me*."

Luxi felt the hair stand on the back of her neck. "Then you meant to . . . to fuck me the whole time?"

He shrugged. "Well, yeah. That's what seduction generally means."

She sucked in a sharp breath and her cheeks flushed with heat. It had been a trick from beginning to end. "Goodbye Leto." She turned and fled the tram.

Luxi strode across the tram station deck toward the lifts on the far wall, moving buoyantly through the low gravity as though through water. She shook her head in painful humiliation. She couldn't believe she had been tricked so easily!

"Luxi!"

Oh Glory, he's yelling for me. Luxi hurried as much as the low gravity would allow. If she could get to the lifts, it would be easy to disappear; this was a big station . . .

She was jerked to a halt by a hand gripping her wrist. *Shit.*

"Luxi."

She turned to look up at Leto. "What now?"

Leto caught her face in his palms and took her mouth in a swift kiss.

She hesitated, he tasted so good . . . She jerked her mouth from his and stepped back. "What was that for?"

Leto licked his lips and his mouth set in a hard smile. "You *do* want me."

Her cheeks heated painfully. "So? Why do you care? You already got what you were after."

Leto raised his chin and set his hands on his hips. "I want more."

"Too bad for you! I'm leaving, remember?" Her knuckles whitened on her bag's tow-handle.

"Not immediately, we still have time . . ."

"No. Absolutely not."

Leto's lips lifted in a sly smile. "I seduced you once, I can do it again."

She jabbed her finger at him. "*You* are a beast! A sneaky, conniving, lying beast!"

"You know me so well!" He grinned shamelessly.

Luxi turned on her heel and stomped into the open lift.

His laughter burned in her ears.

Luxi stepped out of the lift and into gravity feeling exhausted. The broad green bands on the walls told her that she had finally reached the hallways in the Garden district. It took her several minutes of walking before she was used to moving in real gravity again. Sticky, sweaty and tired, she stopped at the first fully equipped facility she found. Luckily it was only a few minutes walk away from the lift.

She shoved through the door with a groan of relief. The tastefully appointed scrupulously clean facility was huge. There was an entire wall of commode stalls and another whole wall of proper water sinks. It was also completely empty. Apparently, this facility didn't see very many people. A door at the far end led to the bathing part of the facility. The long room was lined with small single occupant vibro-shower stalls.

In one of the small private cubicles, Luxi stripped out of her clothes, leaving them draped over the low bench against the wall. With a heavy sigh, she activated the sonic projection in the stall and the antibacterial lighting winked on. She left the small stall no longer sweaty and sticky, but somehow, she just didn't feel clean. She knew she was cleaner than any water shower could get her, but she never *felt* clean without water.

She shoved her soiled clothes into her bag, stepped into fresh panties and then her dark green jumpsuit. She was going to have to find a laundry facility sometime soon. She only had three ship-suits and the green one was her last clean suit. She fastened the suit closed and pulled out her brush to do battle with the snarls from her red mane.

Everything that had happened since she woke up this morning had really taken a toll on her hair. The shuttle flight in zero-g, the tram station's low gravity, the tram—the sex . . . A flash of heat stirred in her belly.

Leto's handsome face suddenly filled her thoughts. His kisses had tasted so clean. His ghost had felt so warm and firm, yet oddly like velvet under her fingers. And the way it felt when he'd touched her, exciting her to the breaking point and finally, taken her . . .

She was not going to see him again. Regret stabbed through her heart.

Luxi took a deep steadying breath and focused on her snarled curls. *Pay attention to what you have to do, not on what you can't have.* Still, she was glad that she had shared that with him. If she failed to find the future she was looking for, and actually reached her final destination, Leto's kisses were going to be the only brightness in a very long and lonely life.

But her talent for reading the future had led her straight to him.

She frowned. Was it possible that he was actually part of her future? She sighed heavily. She didn't see how. He was not the type that worked anywhere near an office.

The image of the cyborg in a business suit suddenly came to mind.

She smiled and shook her head. Not a chance. He was . . . what he was, and she was a receptionist in need of a job. It just wasn't possible that he was a part of her future.

After a long and frustrating struggle, she was finally able to twist the wavy mass up into a tight coil and fasten it with her silver clip. Neat and tidy at last, she stepped into her half-boots and closed her bag. It was time to find that kafé.

And her next appointment with the future.

CHAPTER SIX

Luxi pushed through smoked glass doors and came out of the green-banded corridors onto a railed walkway that bordered on a living forest. Full-sized Terran maple trees over-arched the walkway. They grew from rich earth beds only one story straight down. Live birds called and flew among the branches.

She turned left, heading station south, alongside the forest, towing her hand-bag. Forests, gardens, and fields of crops filled the station's distant curving sides, then climbed up and over the arching ceiling, held firmly rooted by the station's spin-generated gravity. Thin streaks of cloud and passenger shuttles flew upside down across a forest four kilometers away and directly over her head.

A catwalk opened up on her right, leading right through the forest's heart. A posted sign indicated that the Concourse was located at the other end. According to the station flyer, most of the kafés could be found in the Concourse area.

Perfect. She smiled and completely enchanted headed down the catwalk through the arching trees.

The Concourse was like any other interstellar shopping mall with rows of exotic shops along a thoroughfare with potted trees and decorative benches scattered everywhere. There wasn't an enormous amount of foot traffic, but what there was, was very colorful. She spotted dozens of different alien races shopping, eating and chatting, along with various human races from all over the Imperium.

Mixed among the shops were a number of crowded kafés, but according to her talent, none of them were where she was supposed to be. With a heavy sigh, Luxi kept walking.

As she reached the far end of the Concourse, the station lights dimmed into station sunset, and then station night. Tall archaic lamp posts of black iron winked on to provide lighting. Overhead, thousands of tiny lights flickered to life, acting as stars in the completely contained world.

The Pouting Mermaid Kafé sat on the very edge of the upper gallery overlooking the formal gardens two stories below. The shop itself was little more than a fancifully nautical roofed counter framed by a pair of potted dwarf-oaks.

A dozen or so small round tables were scattered by the balcony for relaxing patrons, of which there was only one. A young man in a steel gray floor-length informal coat lounged casually at one of the tables under the golden glow of a lamppost. He held a cup in one gloved hand and a small fiction-reader in the other.

Within her, chance entwined with opportunity. She had arrived at the right place.

Luxi strode for the counter and pulled out her data card. She was simply dying for a cup of kaffa.

The young man behind the counter was busily cleaning one of the antique kaffa brewers that lined the back wall. Artistic cups and mugs perched in nooks on the side walls. He glanced up and smiled. "Hi, I'm Brett, what can I get you?" He was perfectly ordinary. Brown hair, brown eyes, and a slightly rumpled green apron covered his black shirt and trousers.

"Hi Brett, I'm Luxi." She grinned and gave him her order.

Brett grabbed a huge green mug from the wall and started his machines. "So, Luxi, what brings you to Port Destiny?"

Luxi gave him a sour smile. "Just passing through, but I was wondering, would you mind if I borrowed one of your tables to do some fortunetelling?"

Brett glanced over at her, his eyes wide. "Fortunetelling? Here?"

Luxi bit her lip. "Is there a rule against it?"

Brett gave her a sour smile. "No, it's just that most of the other fortunetellers hit the kaffa shops closer to the middle of the Concourse." He poured a liberal amount of cream in the green mug then filled it with freshly brewed black kaffa. "You any good?"

Luxi grinned. "Better than most."

Brett handed her the steaming mug and lifted his brow. "Sure about that, are you?"

Luxi took the cup in both hands. The hot brew smelled heavenly. "Let's put it this way, my talent got me fired from my last job as an information leak, and I was only the receptionist."

"Whoa . . ." Brett blinked. "You must be a major talent."

Luxi shrugged. "I have no idea. Unlike normal psi-talents, this one doesn't show up under testing." She smiled. "Want to test it yourself?"

Brett's mouth fell open. "Me? Oh, hell yeah!"

"Pardon me."

"Huh?" Luxi turned and nearly dropped her cup. The young man in the long gray coat stood by her left elbow with his hands tucked behind him. His eyes were as green as the leaves on the trees and seemed brilliant against the deep auburn red of his tightly bound hair. The long tail falling over his breast and nearly to his waist was bound in a steel gray ribbon nearly to the end, as though to hide the deep fiery color. His face was strongly but arrestingly carved though he seemed young. And his mouth . . . He had the fullest most kissable lips Luxi had ever seen.

He quirked up a dark red brow and smiled at Luxi. "May I observe your work?"

Luxi nearly staggered from the effect. *Whoa, that smile should have a warning label.* She swallowed to get her voice back. "That's up to Brett. It's his fortune."

Brett grinned. "Sure, I don't mind. Want a refill while you're here?"

The young man turned to Brett. "That would be wonderful. And if I may, please put the young lady's order on my tab."

Luxi felt the tiniest shiver. The young man's voice was surprisingly deep and flavored with a rich exotic accent. He had one of those voices that could recite a grocery list and sound compelling.

He turned to Luxi. "You don't mind, do you?"

"Yes, please! I mean no, I mean thank you." Luxi felt her cheeks heat. It was hard to think past that lethal of his smile.

"You are quite welcome." He gave her a small bow. "I am Amun Verity."

She set her cup on the counter and summoned her best manners. With her hands open and correctly placed on her thighs, she gave him a slightly deeper bow in reply, acknowledging his obviously superior rank. She bit back a smile. Everyone was superior to a receptionist. "I'm honored by your acquaintance, gentle sir. I'm Luxi Emory."

Amun grinned unexpectedly. "Was I that formal?"

Luxi bit her lip and shrugged. "It seemed the right thing to do."

Amun shook his head and his smile shifted to something more relaxed.

"Okay . . ." Brett glanced from Luxi to Amun. "Can I have my fortune now?"

Luxi turned to Brett with a grin and picked up her mug. "Absolutely, what would you like to know about, a person, a place or a situation?"

Brett frowned. "Do you need a name?"

"Nope, just a teeny clue; like . . . my girlfriend, my friend, my boss, work . . . Stuff like that."

"Oh, that's it?"

"Yep." Luxi was well aware that her smile was smug. "I told you, I'm good."

Brett leaned both elbows on the counter. "My girlfriend. We're having problems."

Luxi turned her head to stare at nothing in particular and reached for her talent. Her inner sight bloomed allowed her to view the tangled threads of Brett's previous choices and future possibilities. Luxi nodded absently as his story formed then turned to face him. "Okay, this is what's going on . . ." She began to recite what the threads told her about his situation with his girlfriend.

Luxi finally stopped to sip her kaffa.

"Oh wow . . ." Brett stared at Luxi. "Dead on the money!"

"Very impressive."

Luxi started. Amun had been so still, she had forgotten that he was standing right there. She darted a glance his way and froze.

Amun's green gaze was intensely focused, and his smile tight. There was a subtle edge to his expression, as though he had found something truly interesting — and edible. "That is quite a talent."

Luxi swallowed her kaffa and hoped that the heat of her embarrassment didn't show. "Thanks." She cleared her throat and tore her gaze from Amun. If she kept looking at him, she'd fall into his green gaze and forget what she needed to say. She gathered her thoughts and focused on the lines of possibility around Brett. "Okay, now that you know what happened, this is how you fix it . . ."

Brett refilled Luxi's kaffa and set down a plate with one of their signature desserts. "It's on me." He shook his head. "Wow."

"Thank you!" Luxi took her refilled cup and raised her

brow. "I told you I was good."

Brett rolled his eyes. "Good does not even begin to describe what you just did."

Luxi sipped her fresh kaffa to cover her smile. It was nice to actually deliver good news for a change. "So, I can borrow a table?"

Brett gave her a sour smile. "Sure, I'll just move a few patrons out of your way." He waved his hand at the empty tables. "I honestly don't know how much money you're going to make here. Tresday nights are usually quiet, but I'll keep you in kaffa for as long as you're here."

"Thank you." Luxi smiled. "It'll be okay. I only need to make enough for dinner."

"In that case . . ." Amun bowed slightly to Luxi. "For the price of dinner, I would be honored if you would be so kind as to use your talent to view a situation I find myself in a dilemma over."

Luxi grinned up at Brett. "There, you see?" She turned to Amun and returned his less formal bow. "I'd be honored to be of service." She suddenly shivered as the last thread of synchronicity suddenly fell into place. Luxi blinked up at Amun. She was only a breath away to escaping her doom. She had one more decision to make to achieve it.

And Amun was the key.

Amun's gaze sharpened. "What is it?"

Luxi felt a stillness wash through her as she gazed into his green eyes. "I felt the lines of my own fate changing." It was the absolute truth—and she wanted to swallow the words as soon as she said them.

Amun turned and gestured toward his table by the balcony with one gloved hand. "With your level of talent?" He smiled. "I don't see why not."

Luxi picked up the plate and the cup. Why the hell had she told him that? She shook her head as she walked toward his table. *Too late now.*

Amun held out a chair for her then carefully stepped back.

Luxi caught his cue and deposited her plate and cup on the table. She turned to give him a bow in thanks and sat.

Amun smiled and his brow quirked up. "You have very nice protocol for a receptionist." He gathered the long skirts of his gray coat and sat in the chair on her immediate left.

"Oh, that?" Luxi lifted her shoulder in a small shrug and turned away. He was making her blush again. "The company had a number of off-world customers, so I brushed up on their etiquette."

Amun smiled. "Were they surprised?"

Luxi raised a brow. "I thought they would be, but it was more like they expected it."

Amun nodded. "Then you did it right." He raised a finger. "The only time manners are truly noted is when they are missing."

"Oh . . ."

Amun leaned back in his chair and lifted his cup. "Now then, I have two parties in contention trying to come to an accord. I would dearly like to know the results of their interaction."

Luxi set down her cup and gazed over his shoulder to clear her mind and view his synchronicities. She felt her sense of perspective shift hard as his choices and decisions flooded her mind with snarl after snarl of complicated threads that raced from the past to the future. She grabbed hold of the table and sucked in a breath as she tried to find the center, the 'now' that he occupied.

"Is something wrong?" His voice was soft.

Luxi squinted as she fought through tangle after tangle to find him. "Not wrong, just really complicated." She found his center and began her search for the parties he was inquiring about within the two enormous snarls connected closely to his line. Suddenly she realized that both parties were, in fact, the snarls. "Oh, wow . . . big."

Slowly, and carefully, Amun took off his gloves. "Is that so?" he reached out a finger and brushed the side of her hand. "Tell me."

Luxi swallowed. "There's lot there. Do you want their immediate decisions or the possible outcomes?"

"There is only one immediate decision I'm interested in, the one connected directly to me. Find that one decision and follow it to its outcome."

Luxi found the specific thread, followed it, and spoke.

Luxi was shaking as she finished. She let the inner-vision go and reached for her kaffa. Then she noticed that Amun was holding her left hand. Her brow rose. *Okay . . .*

A strong shiver rocked her, and everything she had told him slipped right out of her head. She didn't think anything of it. Memory loss of her readings was normal. The information she revealed was not hers to know, so it simply slipped away. Though never quite that quickly.

Amun's gaze narrowed. "Do you remember any of what you just told me?"

Luxi stopped with her cup halfway to her lips. "Not a thing. All I remember is a really big and tangled mess. Do you need me to go back and look?"

Amun smiled gently as he released her hand. "No, no that won't be necessary. I have everything I need."

"Good." Luxi let out a breath. "*You* are a tough read." She sipped her kaffa. It had cooled quite a bit, but it was still heavenly.

Amun leaned back, quirked up a brow. "You found me difficult?"

Luxi shook her head. "Not difficult; you just had a lot more than I was used to seeing."

"I dare say . . ." Amun smiled and rose from his chair. "I

believe I owe you dinner?"

"Thank you." Luxi rose with a smile. "But I'm afraid I don't know any of the restaurants."

Amun tilted his head, and the golden lamplight gilded his handsome face with gold and shadows. "Actually, I was thinking perhaps of someplace a bit more private."

Private? Luxi felt the slightest touch of alarm slide down her spine. "What exactly do you mean by 'private'?"

Amun smiled warmly. "I find myself wishing to share your company." His gaze focused on her. "You don't mind, do you?"

Luxi was caught by the arresting green of his eyes and the luscious curve of his utterly kissable mouth. Did she mind? Really?

CHAPTER SEVEN

Amun reached out to take both Luxi's hands and gently tugged her closer. "There is a quality about you that is not found in many people. Some would find it irresistible."

Irresistible . . . All rational thought was suddenly consumed by a violent rush of erotic heat. Her pulse suddenly throbbed in her throat, and her nipples tightened to burning points. The firestorm of searing physical need stole her breath.

"Luxi . . ." Amun lowered his head.

Luxi lifted her chin, consumed by the absolute hunger to taste him. Softness brushed against her lips, then pressure . . . She opened to his mouth, and her eyes closed. The moist touch of his tongue brushed hers and took possession. He tasted of expensive kaffa and rich cream with a hint of spice. His hands were so warm.

"Yes," he whispered against her mouth. "Oh yes . . ." He freed one of her hands and slid his arm around her waist, pulling her up against him. He angled his head, and his tongue swept hers boldly, urgently, encouraging her to taste him more fully.

She moaned softly and answered his unspoken command with strong parries of her tongue against his. Her free arm went around his hips. His coat was soft under her fingers. His body was warm, lean, and hard, against hers. His scent was clean and richly flavored with masculine arousal. And unbearably exciting.

He curled her captured hand between them at her heart then lifted his hand from her waist. The clip in her hair was tugged free, and her mane tumbled to her waist in a riot of unbound curls. His finger slid under the heavy mass, and he groaned. He grasped a handful at the base of her neck.

An illicit bolt of brutal excitement stabbed straight down, and moisture dampened her panties. Luxi gasped. Her fingers clenched in his coat and she pressed eagerly against the firm ridge of his erection that rubbed enticingly against her hip.

His fingers tightened in her hair, holding her still as he lifted his lips from hers. He smiled. "You like this," he whispered. "You like being captured, being . . . taken."

She trembled in his firm hold. She couldn't think past the fire that throbbed in her core, not even to agree. She shifted, and the erection under his loose trousers nudged between her thighs. Want and need raked through her. She could not stop herself from rubbing against him.

Amun smiled and brushed his lips lightly, teasingly against hers. "Oh, you are going to be so much fun."

"Amun, what are you doing out of your suite? It's not safe."

Amun abruptly pushed away from Luxi.

Luxi gasped as her mind suddenly returned to her in a tangle of heat and confusion. What had just happened?

Amun blushed and frowned past her shoulder in annoyance. "Your timing is utterly inconvenient."

"So I see." A tall man in a dark suit strode past Luxi toward Amun. A long tail of distinctive silver hair fell to the center of his back. He came to a sudden stop and turned around. His steel gray eyes widened then narrowed. His face was cast in deep shadows under the lamplights, but there was no mistaking who he was. "Well, hello, Luxi. Cheating on me already?"

Leto? Luxi winced and turned away in painful embarrassment. Fate and Glory, it figured . . . The only two men she'd kissed in several cycles *would* know each other.

Amun frowned at Leto. "You know Luxi?"

"Quite well, actually." Leto's smile was thin and sharp. "We shared a tramway car."

Oh, you bastard . . . Her cheeks heated with a sudden rush of hot memory.

Amun peered at Luxi, and his brows rose. "I . . . see."

Luxi scowled at the deck. There was simply no way to explain her actions. Fine then, she wouldn't bother. She lifted her chin and held out her hand to Amun. "My hair clip please?"

"Of course." Amun reached into his pocket and placed the clip in her palm. His fingers brushed hers and heat shimmered from his touch.

Luxi shivered just slightly and pulled her hand away. She took a wary step back from both men and began the task of coiling her hair back up.

"So, Amun, were we having fun?" Leto's voice dripped with sarcasm.

Amun lifted his chin and folded his arms across his chest. "You realize that you are embarrassing Luxi?"

"I'm trying to embarrass you!" Leto took a step closer to Amun and his mouth thinned to a hard line. "You think I don't know what you were doing?"

Amun looked away.

Leto's hands tightened to fists. "That better be guilt I'm seeing."

Luxi frowned. What was going on? From the way Leto was glaring and the way Amun refused to look at him, you would think they were . . . lovers. "So, just how well do you two know each other?"

"Not nearly well enough." Amun shot a narrow glare at Leto.

"Amun, if you want me to play villain, you know better than most that I am very qualified for the part." Leto lowered his brows and folded his arms. "Are you ready to go back?"

Amun stared fixedly at Luxi. "I will do so when I have what I seek."

Leto's mouth curled in a tight smile. "Did you try asking?"

"This? From you?" Amun raised a sarcastic brow at Leto. "Did *you* ask?"

Leto scowled then sighed. "You have a point." His hands dropped to perch on his hips and he nodded at Luxi. "Amun, is my employer."

Luxi choked. "He's your *employer*?"

Amun snorted. "However, there seems to be some doubt as to who is actually in charge."

Leto rolled his eyes. "Luxi, I need to get him back to the suite. Why don't you come with us?"

Amun started tugging on his gloves. "I would be most obliged, and I do owe you dinner."

"Go to your suite?" Luxi crossed her arms. "What? So you can both seduce me?"

Leto pursed his lips and lifted his chin toward Amun. "Well, yes."

Luxi blinked. "You're admitting it?"

Leto shrugged. "I tell the truth on occasion."

"Don't believe a word." Amun suddenly smiled. "He's the one being in the entire Empire that can actually lie to a professional telepath."

"You would know." Leto snorted. "Since you're one of them."

Luxi reeled in shock. Amun *is a professional grade telepath?* She sucked in a sharp breath. So that's what had happened. Amun had used his telepathic talent to magnify her attraction to him into full-blown sexual obsession. She aimed a glare at Amun. "You rolled my mind—you sneak!"

Amun winced and turned away.

"Sneaky does not begin to describe him." Leto's smile

broadened. "Amun has control issues."

Amun raised a brow at Leto. "You don't seem to mind my 'control issues'."

Leto snorted. "Says you."

Amun lowered his gaze. "Am I so terrible a master?"

Leto sighed. "No, you're not terrible. I've had terrible." He raised his chin. "But then I can resist your mind-control tricks — unlike Luxi."

Luxi lifted her chin and folded her arms. "So, why did you roll me?"

"You were already attracted to me." Amun shrugged. "And I wanted you." His chin lowered and he focused on Luxi. "I still do."

Luxi felt a touch of pull from his gaze and hastily averted her eyes. Glory and Fate, he was impressively strong. She was normally resistant to telepaths. "Do you mind?"

"My apologies." Amun smiled sourly. "And don't be impressed. Knowing exactly what someone thinks of you at all times can be very tiring."

Leto grinned. "That's why he runs around with me. He can't read a thought in my head."

Amun raised a brow. "As if you *had* a thought in your head to read?"

Luxi bit her lip. "Try knowing what will happen with every decision you make."

Amun tilted his head and his brows rose. "You do possess quite a talent."

Luxi raised her brow and smiled in spite of herself. "Want to trade?"

"That's not the only talent she has . . ." Leto moved to Luxi's side and caught her wrist. "Amun, take her hand. I want to try something."

Luxi glanced at Amun and tugged at her captured hand. "Leto!"

"Relax. He's not going to roll you." Leto raised a brow at Amun. "Is he?"

Amun sighed and pulled off his gloves. "I will endeavor to restrain myself."

Luxi gave in with a heavy sigh. "Fine, whatever . . ." It wasn't as if she had anywhere near the strength to break the cyborg's grip.

Amun closed his warm fingers around Luxi's hand. "What is it?"

Leto released Luxi's wrist and moved behind her to drop his hands on her shoulders. "Tell me what you feel."

Amun frowned. "All right . . ."

Luxi felt Leto's warm, familiar body pressed tight against hers. She couldn't help the curl of pleasure that arose in her.

Leto set his chin on Luxi's shoulder. His breath was warm in her ear. "Missed me?"

Luxi snorted. "You wish."

Amun lifted his chin. "I'll have you know, she just lied."

Luxi ground her teeth. "Amun!"

Leto chuckled. "Oh, I know."

Luxi felt Leto's arms slide down to wrap around her waist in a snug embrace, even though his hands were still gripping her shoulders. She sucked in a breath and looked down. She could see a pair of colorless arms around her. They had only the slightest haze about them, so they appeared a little indistinct, but they felt incredibly solid. They were from his spirit—his ghost.

Amun licked his lips. "Are you perhaps holding her around the waist?"

"Yes." Leto stared hard at Amun. "You can feel that?"

"Actually, I think I can see it." Amun frowned. "Now that *is* interesting."

Leto's arms tightened around Luxi. "Can you feel me at all?"

Amun's frown deepened. "Yes . . . yes, I do, as though there are two of you, one inside the other. I can almost grasp . . ."

"That's my spirit—my ghost." Leto grinned. "You're a telepath, but you can't read me. Luxi is sensitive to ghosts so we can feel each other. When you read her, you pick me up in the process."

Amun raised a dark red brow. "Fate and Glory, she's a conduit!" He raised a brow at Leto then focused on Luxi. "I'm beginning to suspect that Luxi is a major talent."

Leto's smile was predatory. "She's definitely strong enough to act as a buffer between us."

Amun froze, his wide gaze locked on Leto. "You mean you're willing to . . ."

Leto smiled. "I'm more than willing if you are."

Amun's brows lowered and he smiled. "I can't wait."

Luxi frowned. "What are you two talking about?"

"Sex," both men answered as one. Abruptly they laughed.

Luxi glanced from one to the other. "You mean you haven't . . ."

"Only once." Amun hand tightened on hers. "When we first met."

Luxi raised a brow. "Once?" She didn't see how that was possible. Both of them seemed overwhelmingly determined when it came to getting laid. "Nothing since?"

Amun pinned Leto with a hard stare. "He's afraid of hurting me."

Leto glared right back. "The one time we did, I nearly killed you!"

Luxi frowned. Leto's ghost fed on the energy generated by orgasm. She had barely felt him when he fed from hers, but that was after three other people had already climaxed. How much did he need?

Amun raised his brow. "If I remember correctly, you were

trying to kill me at the time."

Luxi blinked. "He was trying to kill you?"

Amun shrugged. "Assassin was Leto's previous profession." He bit his lip. "I seduced him."

Assassin? Luxi's mouth fell open. "He was . . . you *seduced* an assassin?"

"I woke up to find a very handsome man sitting right on top of me." Amun smiled. "How could I resist?"

"I don't know how he did it, but he . . . rolled me." Leto turned away. "And then my hunger took over. I nearly drained him dry."

"I recovered." Amun's tone was very dry.

Leto ground his teeth. "After three days of almost full body contact!"

Amun smiled. "I wasn't complaining."

Leto rolled his eyes and sighed.

Luxi frowned. "Leto, if you were trying to kill him, why didn't you?"

Leto's arms tightened around her. "I changed my mind." He shot a narrow look at Amun. "Though sometimes I seriously wonder why."

Amun nodded at Luxi. "Now he's in my employ, as my personal bodyguard."

"Bodyguard—my ass!" Leto shot a glare at Amun. "I'm more like a nanny! I leave you alone for an hour and you sneak out to a completely undefended public area!"

Amun's brows lowered and his hand tightened on Luxi's. "You could have stayed."

Leto's eyes narrowed. "You knew damned well that I needed to hunt. If I didn't, my needs would have driven me to feed on you!"

Amun focused past Luxi's shoulder. "Leto."

Leto scowled, meeting his gaze. "What?"

Amun lifted his chin. "You are not the only one with

appetites."

Luxi felt a spear of heat pass right through her heart to dive straight into Leto. She gasped.

Leto stiffened. "Amun?"

The distinct ridge of a sudden and firm erection pressed against the cheeks of Luxi's butt. Leto was hard, and getting harder. Her panties dampened with a spat of cream.

Amun's eyes narrowed as he smiled. "I said that I would not roll Luxi, you on the other hand . . ." He stepped in close. "I intend to show no mercy."

"Amun, I already agreed." Leto swallowed hard. "You don't need to do it this way."

"Perhaps not. Let's just say that I am not in the mood to take chances on you becoming suddenly distracted." Amun's hands slid up Luxi's arms to her shoulders until he brushed Leto's hands. "I have waited long enough." His fingers tightened over Leto's, pressing both their hands into Luxi's shoulders. "I want you." He focused on Luxi. "I want you both."

Lust rolled up from Luxi's belly in a hot thick syrupy fog. It wasn't coming from Amun; it was her body's reaction to the scent of warm leather laced with the rich perfume of two aroused males.

Amun took that last step, closing the distance and pressing Luxi back with his hips, locking her between their warm firm bodies, and their hard cocks. Amun's hands slid down to Leto's hips, embracing them both.

Luxi could barely breathe past the heat rolling through her. Leto's cock was a thick hot bar against her butt. Amun's cock was a broad prod against her belly. Her clit throbbed with heat and her core clenched in hunger. She suddenly desperately wanted to spread her legs a little wider, to give both their cocks room between her thighs, to give them access and let them in.

Amun's gaze narrowed on Luxi. He reached for the clip in

her hair and pulled it free. Her red curls uncoiled and flowed over her left shoulder and Leto's arm. He pocketed the clip. Both men leaned down to press their noses in her unbound hair.

It was painfully erotic. She leaned her head back against Leto's shoulder, and her eyes closed, biting her lip to hold back her moan.

"Luxi."

She opened her eyes to find Amun's green gaze locked on hers. He leaned close and his lips brushed hers. She opened for him and his tongue swept in, taking her mouth in a hungry kiss. She couldn't have stopped her moan if she'd tried.

Leto drew in a deep breath and his hands tightened around her.

Amun released her mouth with a soft smile. His gaze shifted Leto. He leaned past Luxi, and brushed his mouth against Leto's.

Leto opened his mouth to receive Amun's kiss and groaned. His spirit hand slid up from Luxi's waist to cup her breast.

She sucked in a breath. She could feel his hand passing through the cloth of her suit caressing her bare skin as though it didn't exist but was warm flesh.

Leto groaned into Amun's mouth and tugged on her nipple.

Erotic lightning stabbed downward to her clit. Her core throbbed hungrily, and she shifted restlessly between them.

Amun's hips pressed tighter against her, and he shifted, grinding the erection behind his loose trousers against her softness until it nudged between her thighs and up against her clit.

Behind her, Leto shifted against her butt, his cock hard and insistent, but she was pressed too tightly between them.

Amun pulled back, releasing Leto's mouth. He licked his

lips with his hooded gaze focused on Leto.

Leto gasped for breath, and his body trembled as hard as Luxi's.

"Good." Amun reached up to grab the hair at Luxi's neck and the base of Leto's silver tail. "Let's all take a walk, shall we?" He tugged, jerking them both apart to stand on either side of him. "A short walk." He pushed.

They walked.

CHAPTER EIGHT

Amun's grip on their hair was unrelenting as he guided Luxi and Leto across the balcony plaza and into a lift. They stepped within, and he turned them around to face the reflective door. "Ground level."

Leto reached out and pressed the button.

Luxi took a sharp breath. What in Glory had she just gotten herself into? "Amun . . ." The hand tightened in her hair.

"Don't. I can feel the raw lust rolling off you."

Luxi winced. He was right. She was so aroused she was trembling, but some of that was good healthy fear. She'd never been with two men at the same time before. "But, I've never . . ."

"I realize this is all very new for you." Amun's hand loosened in her hair and his smile softened. "We will not be inconsiderate." His glance shifted to Leto. "But I will not be denied."

The lift doors slid back, opening to the deep shadows of the formal gardens.

"Shall we?" Amun's voice was pleasant and firm.

Prodded by the fingers knotted in her hair, Luxi stepped out of the lift cautiously. She couldn't see the ground. Amun's tight hold kept her head up.

Leto was silent and wide-eyed at her side.

They stepped forward into the night enshrouded formal gardens. The flagged path was lined with tall boxed hedges, topiary trees, and small footlights. Crickets sang in the surrounding darkness. The smell of earth and living green perfumed the air. The internal sky was dotted with distant lights that shone like stars.

Amun guided them off the main walk and onto a narrow side path that ran alongside the tall hedges of the maze. He urged them into a sudden turn. They walked into a hedge-walled enclosed alcove with small lights along the ground. A low bench of ornate white marble commanded the very center.

Amun released them. "Disrobe."

Luxi turned to face them, her pulse racing and her mouth dry.

Amun reached for the buttons on his long gray coat. It opened, revealing a long-sleeved dress shirt of charcoal silk. He tossed the coat over the bench and lifted his chin to unbutton his shirt.

Staring at Amun, Leto reached for his fastenings. His shimmering suit parted with incredible speed. Bladed weapons were drawn from hidden sheaths as if by magic. He set them under the bench then sat down to pull off his boots.

Amun slid the charcoal shirt from his shoulders revealing deceptively broad shoulders and a lightly furred chest with nipples tightened to hard points. Deep shadows played across the sleek muscles and defined a slender line of dark hair that trailed down his flat stomach. He tossed the shirt to the ground and reached for the button to his trousers.

Leto stood and pulled the suit from his shoulders revealing ghost-pale skin.

Amun swallowed visibly, his hands frozen on the button to his trousers. "Do you have any idea how truly beautiful you are?" His voice was husky and deep.

Leto smiled. "Am I?" He stripped out of his leather in one long pull. His well-defined arrogantly masculine body and the strong smooth arc of his pale cock glowed in the shadows like sculpted marble.

Oh yes . . . Luxi stared at Leto's incredible form and swallowed hard. *Oh yes, he is . . .* He was blindingly beautiful.

Amun held Leto's gaze and the green of his eyes were thin bands round broad pits of darkness. "What do you think?" His smile was strained. He opened his loose trousers, letting them fall down his strong thighs. His blushing and rigid cock jutted from a discrete nest of dark curls. The graceful curve stretched upward to his navel. He reached down to collect his trousers and dug into the pocket for a small squeeze tube then tossed his trousers over his shirt.

Luxi had to close her mouth. Glory, they were both beautiful. Okay, she was really going to do this. She swept her long mane behind her. Her shaking fingers fumbled with her suit's fastenings. She was out of her mind, but . . .

Leto caught Luxi's hands and tugged her close. "What is taking you so long?" He smiled as he brushed her fingers away from the fastenings.

"I was . . ." Luxi's breath nearly stopped. All that naked magnificence less than a handspan away. She focused on his expressive mouth in helpless fascination and raw yearning.

He focused on her face and his eyes dilated wide, the steel of his eyes barely visible around the dark pit where the shimmer of his ghost dwelled. He lowered his mouth and took her lips in a sudden devouring kiss.

Luxi gladly opened to let him in. His tongue stroked strongly against hers, hot, wet, exciting and hungry. She moaned. His fingers raced down her suit's fastenings and her suit opened. Cool air swept across her skin.

His mouth drifted to her jaw, then lower. His warm hands slid within her suit. "Off, off . . ." His warm breath came in swift pants. His palms drifted down her back, pushing the suit from her shoulders down to her waist. His teeth scored her throat. He impatiently tugged her arms free. His mouth opened on her shoulder and he bit down with bruising force.

Luxi gasped and pushed his shoulder to shove him back. "Leto!"

Leto released her shoulder with a wince. "Sorry," he whispered hoarsely. "I'm having trouble with my control." He knelt and continued to force her suit downward. His clever tongue, soft lips, and nipping teeth explored the revealed flesh of her breasts and belly, drawing shivers and moans. He tugged impatiently until he reached her boots. He lifted her foot.

Luxi grabbed onto his shoulders for balance as her boots were tugged off and tossed. Her suit was dragged all the way down and off.

Leto's hand caught in her panties, tugging them down and off. On his knees, he stared at the ginger curls covering her mound, his gaze wide and dark. He licked his lips and leaned forward.

"Leto."

Leto stopped. He turned on his knees to glare at Amun.

"Patience." Amun, naked and magnificently hard, held out his hand. "Luxi, come here."

Leto stood in one smooth motion.

Luxi crossed her arms and moved past Leto toward Amun.

Amun smiled as he caught at Luxi's hands. "Don't." He pulled them away from her breasts. "You have nothing to be ashamed of." He led her to the white marble bench and spread out his coat. "Straddle it and lie back." He held her hands as she lifted her leg over and sat down, steadying her as she leaned back.

Luxi pulled her hair out from under her and let the red curls spill to the ground. His coat was silky against her back but the bench beneath it was hard stone. It was also far wider than it had looked. She had to spread her legs wide to get her toes to touch the ground. She took a deep breath and glanced over at Amun.

Amun lifted his chin at Leto. "Straddle the bench facing Luxi. This time, you are my mount."

Leto raised his chin and moved to the bench. "No foreplay?"

Amun's lips curled in a sharp smile. "Do you really want another delay?"

Leto focused on Luxi, his mouth tight and his silver eyes still wide and dark. "I see your point."

"Thought you might."

Leto lifted his leg over the bench and sat, then reached down to lift her legs over his spread thighs. He leaned down, grasping the bench on either side of her shoulders. His cock pressed against the curls of her mound as he brushed her mouth with his. "I'll try to be gentle, but I am very close to losing it," he whispered.

Luxi smiled up at him. "That's okay. I'm close to losing it, too."

"One thing more." Humor laced Amun's voice as knelt at their side and held up a gold hoop too small for a bracelet but far too large for a finger ring.

Leto sucked in a breath. "I am *not* . . ."

Amun's smile was predatory as he pushed Leto to sit up. "Yes, you are."

Luxi frowned. "What is that?"

Amun wrapped his hand around Leto's cock and gave it a strong pull. "This is a cock ring." He slid his hand back down and pulled again.

Leto tilted his head back. He gasped, and his hips jerked. "Son of a bitch!"

"It will keep him from climaxing." Amun slid the ring over Leto's thick cockhead, drawing a moan from Leto's lips as he pushed it all the way down to the base of his cock. Amun glanced at Luxi. "At least until I'm ready to let him."

Leto sucked in air past his clenched teeth. "I hate those

things!"

Amun raised a brow. "Really?" He picked up a small tube from where he had set it in the grass and squeezed a thick coating of gel onto his palm. "I find them quite delightful."

Leto glanced at Amun's cock then shot him a narrow glare. "You're not wearing one."

Amun smiled. "Yet." He set down the tube and lifted another gold ring. He grasped his cock with the gel slick palm and stroked himself. "I am in no mood to lose it the moment I have what I have waited nearly a year to get." He coated himself thoroughly with the clear gel then put the ring over his cockhead and slid it down with a groan.

Luxi swallowed and felt a fine tremble run through her. She was going to do this. She was going to have sex with two men. Two of the most beautiful men she had ever seen. She could feel her excitement, her cream gathering and sliding from her body to the coat below her. She pressed her hands over Leto's where they rested on her wide-open thighs.

Amun rose to his feet then strode around to straddle the bench behind Leto. His hands cupped Leto's pale shoulders as he leaned over him. His gaze was hot on Luxi's face. "Mount her."

Leto's gaze widened just a hair and he leaned up then over Luxi. One hand gripped the bench by her shoulder. "Yes, master." His cock slid back across her ginger curls then nudged at her damp and aching flesh.

Luxi felt her breath catch and arched up on instinct alone.

Leto thrust. In a swift voluptuous rush, he sheathed himself fully.

They both moaned.

Amun choked, his eyes widening and his fingers digging into Leto's shoulders.

Luxi rolled her hips under him, feeling the flesh and the spirit within his flesh filling her at once with heat and darkness. She caught his shoulder and pulled him down to her even as she rose from the bench to feel more of him.

Leto dropped down over her, and his mouth took her breast. He sucked greedily on her engorged nipple even as one of his hands slid down to cup her ass cheek.

Luxi moaned scorched by his mouth, his tongue, and his teeth, on her excited flesh.

Abruptly Leto stilled; his entire body tensing.

"Push out," Amun said softly.

Leto's head lifted from her breast and his eyes closed tight. A groan escaped him. He inched forward over her, arching slightly upward.

Above and behind him, Amun's eyes were narrowed to green slits as he sighed. "Yes, oh yes . . ."

Below them, Luxi felt Leto's rigid body rock with impact as Amun sheathed himself in Leto's body.

Leto released a gasp. "Amun, you are not a small man."

Amun groaned. "Nor are you." He thrust. His impact transferred to Leto and drove Leto's cock hard into Luxi.

Luxi gasped and Leto gasped with her.

Amun groaned. "Oh, that was a nice clear impression from both of you."

Leto snorted. "I'm glad you're enjoying your ride in our heads."

"Oh, I am." Amun smiled. "Want to join me?"

Luxi felt the curl of vibrant heat from Amun's mind flooding her with his telepathic impressions. Suddenly she could feel Amun's cock in the hot tight grip of Leto's ass and the wet, slick grip of her own cunt around Leto's cock in addition to the thick delicious fullness of Leto's cock within her. Lust coiled tight within her, compounded by the raging need from both men threaded with the real affection they had for each other. And were beginning to have with her.

"Now that we are all in this together . . ." Amun grabbed

hold of Leto's tailed mane, drawing Leto's head up and back, pulling him upright as he rolled Leto's tail around his fist. "Shall we fuck?"

Leto winced and caught Luxi around the hips. "Amun, I can't . . . Not this way."

Luxi could feel the tension in Leto's body as he strained against the fisted grip in his hair compounded with the physical need to thrust into her body

"You're not." Amun cupped Leto's hip in one hand. "I am doing the fucking." He dug his feet into the grass and pulled, causing Leto to withdraw.

Luxi moaned. Locked in the telepathic link, she could feel the tight, near painful fullness of Amun's cock lodged in Leto's ass along with the bite of his fingers in Leto's hip and then the delicious slow withdrawal mixing with her own pleasure as Leto's cock slid partway from her.

Amun shoved forward driving himself into Leto who drove into Luxi. "I'm fucking the both of you." He pulled back, drawing Leto from Luxi, and thrust again; swifter, harder and deeper . . .

Luxi lifted her hips to receive Leto's driven strokes. She groaned as each hammering thrust struck something deep and delicious within her.

The echoes of pleasure slid from mind, to mind, to mind. Raw animal need rolled over all three of them, bowing them with tension, heat and coiling fire. Sweat formed and slid across heated skin as moans, gasps, and groans filled the small alcove along with the sound of wet flesh striking wet flesh.

Grunting with effort, Amun drove the merciless thrusts that Leto delivered as Luxi writhed beneath them feeling the building tightness of a climax all three were going to share. Whoever climaxed first would set off the cascade into the other two.

And they fucked.

Amun suddenly shoved Leto down over Luxi.

Luxi reached up to clutch at Leto, desperate to feel his skin on hers even as his mouth descended on her breasts in a greedy hunger echoed in both men. Leto's hand gripped the bench over her head as he rocked into Amun's thrusts and let the impact drive him into Luxi's hungry wet core.

And they fucked.

From the heat growing fast in her belly within the echoes of Amun's and Leto's pleasure, compounded by the nips on her breasts and the hard suckling on her nipples, Luxi strongly suspected she would climax very soon.

Amun lifted higher, forcing Leto to lie flat over Luxi, and began to power his thrusts, increasing his speed and depth.

Leto gasped and drove faster into Luxi.

Through the telepathic link, Luxi felt the burn in Amun's balls as his body tried to climax and the snug ring prevented it.

Locked into the link with them, Leto also tried to release and was prevented by his ring.

Luxi felt the sudden clench of her own body notching tighter toward climax. She writhed in vicious pleasure, balanced on the very edge even as both men were driven back from theirs.

And they fucked.

Locked in each other's minds, their shared pleasure drove them upward toward writhing blinding madness. Their moans became gasping cries.

"Enough." Amun groaned at Leto's back. "Send her over."

Luxi shivered at his words.

Leto's hand slid between their bodies. He slicked his fingers in her generous cream, then found her swollen clit. He rubbed, quickly and insistently. His fingers delivered lightning bolts of erotic fire that echoed through all three.

Amun's breath came in harsh pants. "Cum for us. Cum for us all."

Luxi bowed up under them and drew in a breath she couldn't release.

Leto bit down hard on her nipple.

Luxi released her breath on a howl. She exploded in a firestorm of ruthless and rapturous pleasure, feeling her own body's pulsing grip around Leto as she squeezed his cock, begging for his release.

Leto stilled briefly, caught in her climax, then Amun stilled, equally caught. Both men threw back their head and shouted in the ruthless grip of sudden unstoppable release.

The white fire of backwashed ecstasy raged through Luxi's mind, violently hammering her back up and forcing her over into another rolling wave of body-shattering climax, and then another. Her screams echoed their hoarse shouts as she was drowning in the liquid pleasure of both cocks pumping cum into the moist, hot, tight places they were buried.

Something deep and painfully beautiful sparked between both men and arced across the link. Leto leaned back to catch hold of Amun and kissed him. Their mouth worked as the last echoes of climax shimmered around and through them all.

Luxi's sight ran and smeared as tears spontaneously erupted and silently ran down her cheeks. She held her breath to keep from disturbing them as her heart tried to shatter in her chest.

It was love. They were very much in love.

Something she had never felt herself.

Leto abruptly released Amun to lean down over Luxi. He smiled, and kissed her, very, very gently.

CHAPTER NINE

Luxi wiped her eyes and panted, thoroughly worn out as she sprawled beneath Leto's gasping and heavy body. It had been the most brutally erotic thing she had ever experienced. Tremors shook her with tiny echoes of pleasure.

Amun groaned and sat up, leaning his head back with his eyes closed. "Imagine if we had taken the time for foreplay?"

Leto groaned and shifted atop Luxi. "I don't think I would have survived."

Amun stroked Leto's shoulder and groaned. "There is only one way to find out." He sucked in a deep breath and leaned over to one side. "Luxi, are you all right?"

Luxi was barely able to turn her head to look at him. "I think so."

Amun smiled. "How are your administrative skills?"

Her what? Luxi blinked. "Huh?"

Amun lowered his chin, and a chuckle escaped. "Do you have the training to be a personal assistant?"

"Oh . . ." It took two full breaths before Luxi was able to conceive of an answer, never mind verbalize it. "I have the array, and I've done some assistant work."

Amun's smile was wry. "Would you consider being mine?"

Luxi went very still as synchronicity shimmered, stretched high and tight in the back of her mind. "What?"

Leto lifted his head. "He's asking if you want a job." He turned and gave Amun crooked grin. "With us."

Luxi struggled to rise, and Leto caught her by the arms to

help her sit up. She focused on Amun. "Are you serious?"

Amun smiled. "Absolutely."

Leto snorted. "I hope you realize he likes to sleep with his staff?"

Luxi raised her brow at Leto. "No, really?" Her voice was very dry.

Amun's head came up. "Leto!"

Leto reached down to grab his suit. "Well, you do!"

Amun shrugged into his shirt. "Only you."

"Then you don't intend to sleep with your secretary?" Leto nodded at Luxi.

Amun sighed. "You have a point, seeing as I can't sleep with my pilot without her."

Luxi blinked at Leto. "You're a pilot, too?"

Leto shrugged as he rose from the bench. "Pilot, body-guard . . ." He shot a sharp smile at Amun. "Babysitter."

Amun gave him an equally sharp smile. "Lover." He lifted his chin to catch Luxi's eye. "Think carefully. I have a very tight and varied schedule."

Leto grinned. "He means we move around a lot and rarely see anyone but each other for long periods of time."

Luxi glanced down at the grass and then looked up at the winking lights of the distant ceiling. "I never really had much of a social life." She turned to look into Amun's steady green gaze and let her gaze drift over Leto's pale profile. Her choice had been made the moment she took the data card from Gentle-fem Symposia's hand. She hadn't known where it would lead, not really, but a future with these two men was definitely something she could live with. And if she was lucky, perhaps she could acquire a small corner of their hearts, too. She smiled up at Amun. "I think I'd like working for you."

Amun's gaze narrowed on her. "Then you consent to my service?"

Leto peered sharply over his shoulder. "Amun, that's . . ."

Amun shot him a narrow glare. "Don't interfere."

Leto turned away and stepped into his suit.

Luxi's gaze flicked from one to the other. "I consent."

Leto winced.

Amun smiled. "Then by the power I represent, I accept you into my personal attaché."

Leto sighed and smiled tiredly at Luxi. "Welcome to the insanity."

Amun rose from the bench with a groan. "As soon as we get you up to the suite, I'll have you registered and your clearances set."

Leto leaned back and rolled his shoulders. "She needs her translation programs updated, too."

Luxi winced. That was an understatement.

Amun picked up some of his discarded clothing. "I'll see to that and anything else that needs upgrading."

With much groaning and wincing, they dressed.

As they rode the lift back up to the Concourse level, it seemed the most natural thing in the world for Luxi to simply lean against Amun's left side even as Leto leaned against Amun on the right. Luxi felt warm, cozy, and relaxed. More relaxed than she had ever been. She felt . . . safe.

Amun closed his arms about them both, his hand absently stroking Luxi's arm.

The lift doors opened.

Luxi suddenly felt probability snap into actuality with the blow of a hammer. Vincent was somewhere on the station, and he was close—and getting closer with each breath. Possibilities lashed at her. According to what she was reading, Vincent was a danger to both Amun and Leto, but he didn't know them—yet. Despair washed through her. If she stayed with them, Vincent would find them and hurt them. They would be safer if she left them immediately.

Luxi lunged out of the lift at a run. She had to find a place to hide, and fast, but she needed her bag. It was still sitting over by the kaffa house counter where she'd left it.

"Luxi!" Leto shouted from behind her. "Where are you going?" He caught up with her before she'd made it a third of the way across the balcony, grabbing her wrist to jerk her to a halt. "Luxi, wait!"

"Leto, let go!" She turned and tugged at her wrist. "Something came up, I have to go!"

"Luxi, what's wrong?" Amun caught her by the other wrist and hissed. "Who is this man hunting you?"

Luxi flinched. Amun must have plucked the thought from her mind. "His name is Vincent." Her talent spun around her. "Amun, don't let him find you, he can hurt you."

Amun snorted. "I am more difficult to hurt than you think."

"And he'll have to go through me first." Leto grinned nastily.

Luxi stared at him. "Leto, you are in more danger than he is."

Leto's fingers tightened on her wrist. "What?"

"He calls himself a monk. He's possessed by a ghost that devours spirits." She tugged at her arm. "Amun, please, let me go . . ."

Leto frowned. "A monk?"

"Sounds like an Avatar." Amun frowned at Leto. "You could be in real danger."

"An Avatar?" Leto snorted. "Is that all? I've dealt with ghosthunters before."

"Have you now?" The voice was deep and frighteningly familiar.

An icy wash of terror flowed down Luxi's spine.

Amun released her with a gasp.

Luxi turned and froze.

"I've been looking everywhere for you, girl." Vincent

stepped from out the deep shadows, tall and menacing in a floor-sweeping black coat. His shoulder-length sable hair gleamed with streaks of blood-red and his features seemed harsh and barbaric under the lamplight. His eyes had deep smudges from sleepless exhaustion under them and writhing shadows within them. His smile reeked of a feral triumph that did not look natural to his face.

Leto stepped in front of Luxi and Amun. Framed in a pool of light cast by the decorative lampposts, his suit shimmered with midnight rainbows and his hair gleamed with frost. He lifted his chin. "Vincent, I presume?"

Vincent's brows lowered and his chin lifted. "You presume correctly. I'm here for the girl."

Amun moved in front of Luxi and his narrowed his eyes at Vincent. "I'm afraid she's spoken for."

"In that, you are quite correct." Vincent's smile thinned. "I am Avatar Vincent of the Paladin Order, and I will thank you to release my legal property."

Property? Luxi's stared at Vincent's towering and shadowed form in abject horror. "That's impossible!"

Amun bared his teeth in a parody of a smile. "With all due respect, Avatar, Gentle-fem Emory is my employee."

"And I assure you, I have prior claim." Vincent's smiled frosted. "Come Gentle-fem Emory, it's time to go home."

Luxi backed a step away. "What do you think I am, stupid?"

Vincent's smile disappeared completely. "Don't make me come get you."

Two blades appeared in Leto's hands from nowhere. "You'll have to go through me first." He smiled.

Luxi sucked in a sharp breath. Leto was impressively fast. They were going to defend her — against Vincent? No one had ever defended her from anything. It was better business to abandon the problem and not take sides.

Amun narrowed his eyes at Vincent. "There's something odd going on in Vincent's head. It's as though he is literally of two minds. He seems to be listening to someone else speaking, but I cannot make out what is being said."

Luxi bit her lip. "He does have two minds; if you count the ghost as one of them."

Amun frowned at Luxi. "Then according to what I am overhearing, it's the ghost that actually wants you."

"The ghost wants me?" Luxi shook her head. That didn't make any sense. "What for?"

Amun snorted. "Nothing good, I would suppose."

Vincent glared at Leto then his gaze turned calculating. "You have a ghost. No, you *are* a ghost—housed in a robot."

"I started out as a cyborg actually." Leto's smile gleamed in the shadows. "My body isn't biological anymore, but I actually belong here. You, on the other hand, are a living man possessed by a very dead spirit that isn't yours. It doesn't belong in you at all."

Vincent's mouth tightened. "You have no place in this world. You should return to the dead."

Leto snorted. "I can't return to where I've never been—unlike *your* other half."

Vincent's gaze chilled. "You feed on the living. You have to remain in that body."

"And your ghost doesn't?" Leto raised a dark silver brow. "Or does your ghost feed on *you*?"

Vincent's face flushed with rage, but his voice was quiet. "I will take great pleasure in destroying you."

"Temper, temper . . . So you are feeding your ghost." Leto grinned. "And better monks than you have tried."

Vincent held out his hand. "Come, Luxi. You have caused me enough trouble already."

"No." Luxi backed away another step. "I'm not going anywhere with you."

"The way I see it, Avatar . . ." Amun's mouth tightened. "You seem to be the cause of all the trouble."

Vincent glared at Amun. "You know nothing." He focused on Luxi. "Come here. Do not incur more punishment than you have already earned."

"Punishment?" White hot fury surged up Luxi's spine. "Now wait just a damned minute! Punishment for what?"

Vincent's eyes gleamed in the half-light. "For deserting your lawful master."

"Screw you!" Luxi was so angry she shook with it. "You are not my master in any way, shape, or form!"

Amun's brows shot up. He glanced at Luxi, and a small smile appeared.

"Oh, but I am." Vincent's jaw tightened and took a step closer.

"That is close enough, monk." Leto pointed a serrated blade at Vincent's heart and flipped the other blade expertly in his hand. "But we can argue the *point* if you like."

Amun frowned. "He's lying, but he's not lying."

"What?" Luxi gaped at Amun in shock. "How did you . . ."

"Professional grade telepath, remember?" Amun snorted. "Vincent is projecting loud and fairly clear."

Luxi winced. "Oh . . ."

Vincent's black eyes focused on Leto. "Station security will have something to say about this."

"You think so?" Leto tilted his head to one side. "Ever hear the phrase, rank has its privileges?"

Vincent leaned back just a hair. "What?"

Leto bared his teeth in something that wasn't even close to a smile, and his voice was very soft. "Master forgot to wear his jewelry."

"Avatar." Amun lifted his chin. "What claim do you have on Luxi?"

Vincent lifted his chin. "That is not your concern."

Amun sighed. "Ah . . . He's filed an indenture claim."

"I'm indentured?" Luxi's felt her heart stutter in her chest. She was the legal slave of this monster? How by Glory, had that happened?

"Not yet, but he has filed for it." Amun caught Luxi's shoulder and whispered. "Is your data card secure?"

Luxi touched her breast pocket. "Yes."

"Good." Amun smiled tightly. "You're safe as long as you don't give him your verbal agreement or your card."

Luxi frowned. "He can't access anything on the card."

"He can access your identity, and that's all he needs to complete enough of the process for a legal collection." Amun frowned at Vincent. "Once you're in his hands it's a simple matter of getting a DNA sample from you and his ownership is secured."

Luxi shuddered in icy fear. Vincent was a lot bigger than she was. Getting a verbal agreement out of her wouldn't take much force, and a single hair would carry her DNA. The only thing that really stood between her and that monster was her tiny data card.

Amun smiled at her. "Don't be afraid. I will take care of everything." He caught her gaze. "Kiss me."

Lust, heat, fire and sincere affection rolled over Luxi's mind, emptying her thoughts of everything but an over-whelming hunger to taste him, to feel him . . . She pressed up against his body and kissed him with a soft moan of urgency.

Amun pulled back releasing her mouth with a tight smile.

Luxi's mind returned in a cool rush. She jerked back. "You rolled me!"

"Just a little, to relax you," Amun said softly. "I promise I will keep you safe. Do you believe me?"

Luxi bit her lip. Somehow, she did believe him, and she did feel calmer. She nodded.

Amun smiled. "Good."

Luxi's talent moved in the depths of her mind. The lines of chance and potential fade into one strong line that led into the future. Her final decision had occurred, and she had somehow taken it. She was on the path to her alternate future. And she had no idea what had triggered it.

She scanned the lines of her past. Somewhere she had made a decision, done something, or said something that had allowed it to happen. But for the life of her, she couldn't spot it.

Two station security guards stepped out of the lift. Their dark doublets gleamed with silver shields emblazoned with: Sojourn Corp over their breast pockets and swords graced their hips. One of them lifted their chin. "You requested security, Master Verity?"

Vincent glared at the guards then turned his glare on Leto.

Leto smiled and tapped his temple with a finger. "Told you."

Amun smiled and nodded. "I did. There seems to be a problem with my employee, Gentle-fem Emory."

Luxi's mouth popped open. Amun called security — for her?

Amun's fingers tightened on her arm. "Would you be so kind, as to put Gentle-fem Emory under protective custody until a certain legal dispute has been . . ." He leveled a glare at Vincent. "Settled?"

Protective custody? Luxi rocked on her heels.

"Of course, Master Verity." The guard nodded at Amun the turned to Luxi. "Gentle-fem Emory, this way please?"

Amun pushed Luxi gently toward the guards. "I will see you within the hour."

Luxi took a hesitant step toward the guards and turned back to look at Amun. "But . . ."

Amun leveled a stern look her way. "Go. They will keep you safe."

Vincent's brows lowered over his shadowed eyes as he glared at Amun. "This will gain you nothing."

"Leto, I need to go to my suite." Amun pulled his gloves from his pocket and slid them on, ignoring Vincent. "Immediately."

Luxi folded her arms across her chest as she was escorted by the two sword-wearing guards back across the Concourse balcony to the lift she had just left. She turned toward the door to see Amun and Leto disappearing toward the opposite side of the balcony. Her carry-bag trailed behind in Leto's grasp. She winced. Damnit, she didn't even have her hairbrush.

Vincent was a still and menacing shape that stared after her. Under the strong light of the lamp post, Vincent cast two shadows on the Concourse deck. One of them was the dark bulk of Vincent's body, but the other was smaller, and a completely different shape.

Vincent's ghost was solid enough to cast a shadow.

Luxi shivered hard as the lift doors closed.

CHAPTER TEN

Two levels up Luxi followed the guards out of the lift and onto a walkway that crossed one of the shuttle-ways tunneling throughout the station. Plain steel walls painted with a broad green band arched over her head. Several small four-passenger shuttles zipped up and down the roadway below.

She bit her lip as she followed one guard along the walkway with the other right behind her. *Great, this is just great.* Once again, Vincent had to step in and ruin everything. She crossed her arms and gripped her elbows as she walked. She still couldn't believe that Amun and Leto were so willing to defend her. They hadn't even asked; they just . . . did it. She shook her head. She'd never seen anything like it. In business, you cut your losses; you didn't defend them. Not unless they were valuable.

She sighed. *I'm just a receptionist, not a whole lot of value here.*

Luxi was led around a corner and through a doorway into a small and somewhat empty steel-walled parking garage. A blocky armored security shuttle painted in Sojourn Corp's distinctive black and gold was parked at the bottom of the small staircase.

One of the guards opened the back passenger-side door and assisted Luxi into the back seat. The door was closed and clicked as it locked.

Luxi didn't quite conceal her flinch.

The guards climbed into the front seats without saying a single word. The hover engines whined as it powered up. In a matter of moments, the shuttle lifted on a low cushion of anti-grav and backed out of the parking space then pulled out into the tunnels diving into the light traffic.

Vincent . . . What in Glory was she going to do about him? Luxi stared out the shuttle's window at the endless steel walls and tried to think. Vincent had filed for indenture, but how? She had thought that only someone legally wronged could sue for indenture. It was how businesses recovered their losses from crimes committed by employees. High debt could also result in indenture, but again, it was a monetary loss issue. She knew for a fact that all her debts had been cleared, Gentle-fem Symposia had made very sure of that.

Luxi shook her head. The only other way to be indentured was to volunteer your services. There was no way she'd ever agree to that or turn over her data card. She lifted a hand to her breast pocket. The seal was open.

Ice water slid down Luxi's spine. She shoved her fingers into her pocket. The card was gone. That card had everything: her money, her flight plan, her identity . . . Panicked, she checked every pocket in her suit. Gone.

Had she left it at the counter when she'd bought her kaffa? No, she remembered picking it up. The garden; it had to be in the formal garden. Her pocket must have opened when Leto pulled her suit off to . . . fuck.

She eyed the passing hallways, her hands locked together in her lap to hold back the trembling. Getting back to the garden wasn't going to happen anytime soon. At this point, her only hope was that the cleaning crew would find it and notify her when it was found.

Technically, the data card was perfectly safe. The DNA encryption would not allow anyone to access anything more than a view of her identity. Her tickets and her money were inaccessible to anyone but her.

But if Vincent found a way to get his hands on her card, her identity info would be enough to get her into his custody, and then he would own her — body and soul.

She shivered slightly. Amun had said that it was the ghost that really wanted her. But that didn't make any sense at all. What would a ghost want with her?

The shuttle took a sharp left turn, ramped up into a tunnel, then drove through a security grid without bothering to slow down. They ramped up again onto a two-lane roadway marked by broad silver bands.

Luxi bit her lip. The Silver district was the military level. There was absolutely no way for her to leave it; she didn't have the clearance. But then, Vincent shouldn't have the clearance to enter it either. She hoped.

They drove through another security grid, and gold bands replaced the silver bands on the walls.

Luxi's brows shot up. They put people in custody in the Gold District, the high security zone? She smiled sourly. It made sense. Gold District was harder to get into or out of than Silver. It was highly doubtful that Vincent had the clearance to get near the Gold District.

The shuttle took an off-ramp that led into a small parking lot and parked. The doors opened.

Luxi climbed out of the car then checked the seat, just in case her card had fallen out in the shuttle. It hadn't.

One of the guards took her elbow to guide her. "This way Gentle-fem Emory."

Luxi nodded and followed the guards, clenching her hands together to hold back her panic. A short walk across the parking garage led to a security door. The door opened onto a richly carpeted and broad hall painted with broad gold bands. Five paces into the hall a broad doorway held a buzzing energy grid.

Luxi swallowed hard. That grid could char a living being to dust in seconds.

The guards flanked her, took her by the elbows and

marched her toward the deadly grid without pause. "Stay close to us, Gentle-fem Emory." Between one step and the next, the grid shut down, reactivating at their heels.

One of the guards smiled. "See, that wasn't so bad." She was released. "We're almost there."

Luxi sucked in a breath to get a grip on her leaping pulse. "You keep prisoners in Gold District?"

The guard grinned. "You're not under arrest Gentle-fem Emory, just in protective custody. You'll be staying in a suite."

Luxi nearly tripped. A Gold District suite? Were they joking?

One of the guards stopped at an ornately decorated perfectly round shielded door. He pressed his palm to the lighted box on the right and the door rolled away to reveal a second shielded door rolling the other way.

The hallway was arched and softly lit by decorative frosted glass sconces along the ceiling. Golden light spilled down wine-colored walls onto small carved wooden tables holding tasteful flower arrangements and art objects. The carpet was a deep smoke gray.

The guards stopped at a narrow door. "Here you are." The guard pressed the panel and it opened. "We'll be right outside if you need anything."

"Thank you." Luxi walked in and stopped dead.

The room was expensively decorated in gold-veined marble and cream silks. The walls were a rich, warm cream with deep gold carpeting. Centered on the back wall and right in front of her was a massive bed draped in cream silk and mounded with gold tasseled pillows. Gold velvet curtains cascaded from the ceiling to the floor around the bed. On the far left, a huge mirrored armoire took up most of the wall by the open door to the facility. On the far right, a marble-topped dresser with a massive oval mirror took up a large portion of that wall with a closed door just beyond it.

This was protective custody?

Out of sheer curiosity, she went to the left and into the facility. It not only had a frosted glass enclosed water shower — It had a gold-flecked bathtub large enough to hold four. Thick towels and decanters of soap were laid out on the long counter next to a brush and comb set. A hook by the door showed a fluffy bathrobe in cream velvet and gold satin.

Luxi started pulling off her suit. She wanted to take advantage of that water shower before someone realized that she wasn't supposed to be here and made her leave.

Finally naked, Luxi tossed her clothes on the counter and selected a decanter of liquid soap scented with rich vanilla from the row of colorful squeeze bottles on the counter by the towels. Cautiously, she stepped into the roomy shower stall and turned on the water. Four strong jets sprayed decadent amounts of deliciously hot water, soothing sore muscles before spilling down her body in soul-warming sheets. Her blissful groans echoed in the room as steam curled up around her. And she didn't care.

Luxi slathered herself in soap and took great delight in scrubbing every inch of her body and her hair twice. With great reluctance, she finally turned off the water.

"You know there's another whole bottle of that vanilla soap if you want to continue."

Luxi released a short scream and her feet slid on the slick tiles. She grabbed onto the handrail that circled the shower and whirled around.

Leto leaned against the frame of the shower's open door, grinning. His arms were folded across his marble pale bare chest, wearing little more than knee-high dress boots and sleek velvet tights. "Having fun?"

"Leto?" She shoved wet hair from her cheeks. "How long have you been there?"

"Long enough." Leto shook his head and chuckled. "If this

is what you're like in a shower, I can't wait to see what you're like in a tub."

Luxi frowned. "What are you doing here?"

Leto shook out a fluffy cream towel. "I figured I'd check to see what was taking you so long."

"You knew what room I was in?" Luxi reached for the towel.

Leto dodged her hands and wrapped the towel around her, locking her in a snug embrace. "I should. You're in our suite." He dropped a quick kiss on her lips and ruthlessly proceeded to scrub her skin dry.

Luxi grabbed onto his shoulders to keep from being knocked over. "*Your* suite?"

Leto knelt as he slid the towel up her thighs. "You're in protective custody." He glanced up and grinned. "Our protective custody."

"I am?" Luxi shook her head. "No one said anything."

"Of course not." Leto grabbed a fresh towel from the counter. "We didn't want Vincent to know where you were going." He turned her around and rubbed the towel through her long, wet hair. "By the way, you have a very fine ass."

Luxi felt her cheeks heat. "Thanks."

Leto tossed the towel on the counter and walked past her to open the facility door. "Time to get dressed."

"All right." Luxi reached for her discarded green suit, vaguely disappointed that she wouldn't get to wear the robe.

Leto took two long steps back toward Luxi and snatched the green ship-suit from her hand. "Nope, not that." He tossed the suit back on the counter.

Luxi frowned. "I am not walking around naked."

Leto turned around to face her. "You could . . .?"

"No." Luxi pointed a finger at him. "Absolutely not!"

Leto grinned and set his hands on her shoulders. "Relax. Your clothes are on the bed." He gently but firmly pushed her backwards toward the open facility door. "Well, what we could get for you in a hurry."

Luxi frowned up at him as she walked backwards. "You got me clothes?"

"Of course." He nodded as he pushed her out of the facility. "You can't wear a ship-suit to an Imperial diplomatic conference."

Luxi's bare feet sank into the bedroom's rich carpeting. "What diplomatic conference?"

Amun's voice called out from behind her. "The one I am mediating."

Luxi sucked in a breath and turned around.

Amun smiled. "Liked the shower, did you?" Formal court robes of silver and charcoal draped to his heels. A slender band of silver shimmering with rainbow hues circled his forehead.

Luxi stared in shock. Amun had an Imperial circlet? He was an Imperial Lord?

Leto grinned as he pushed Luxi toward the bed. "I was convinced she was doing more than washing."

"So was I. I was beginning to feel left out." Amun lifted a shift of nearly transparent cream silk from the bed. "Hands up, we need to get you dressed so we can begin your downloads."

Too shocked to resist, Luxi stood before Amun and put her hands up. The shift was dropped over her head and a white silk robe was lifted from the bed. In very short order, Amun and Leto had folded and tied the floor-length robe around her. Between them, they arranged a heavier robe of gold-trimmed cream over the white robe, tied with a broad gold velvet sash snug under her breasts and knotted at her back. Matching velvet slippers were set on her feet.

Amun waved his hand at the deep cream hooded robe that was still on the bed. "We'll save that for when it's time to leave." He turned her toward the open door by the dresser. "Your upgrades await you."

Luxi felt her cheeks heat. "Um, guys? How about some underwear? You know panties?"

Leto snorted as he knelt and fussed with the folds at her back. "You won't need them."

Luxi's mouth fell open. "What!" She looked over her shoulder at Leto. "I'm a girl!"

"We had noticed that," Amun said dryly.

Leto tugged at the bows at her side. "The robes are floor-length no one will see anything."

Luxi gripped the silk. "But I'm not . . . I don't . . . You just don't go around without underwear!"

"Are you kidding? Under heavy court robes?" Leto bit back a grin as he stood up. "It's done all the time."

Luxi almost stomped her foot. "But I don't!"

Amun covered his mouth with his hand and closed his eyes briefly. "Unless you bring attention to it, no one will be the wiser."

"You're not serious?" Luxi's fingers tightened on the robes. "No underwear?"

Amun lowered his chin. "Mind your hands, don't crease the silk."

Luxi released the robes and tucked her hands behind her. "Amun, I don't walk around without underwear!"

Amun rolled his eyes. "You'll survive an evening without panties, I promise." He caught her shoulders and turned her toward the open door by the dresser. "We have much to accomplish and not much time to accomplish it." He gently but firmly pushed her toward the next room. "Go."

Leto stepped into the room ahead of them, not even bothering to hide his chuckles.

The next room was enormous and done in black marble and silver with deep scarlet carpeting. The monstrous bed commanding the center of the back wall was twice the size of hers and draped in black velvet. A massive black marble and smoked glass desk took up one entire corner.

Leto picked up a short silk robe of deep black from the edge of the bed and shrugged into it. "Is this going to take long?"

"That depends on Luxi's download speed and how many files she needs." Amun walked to the desk and turned the black leather chair toward Luxi. "Sit here." He leaned over the desk to pick up a data feed cord.

Luxi gathered the robes and sat carefully in the leather chair. The rich silk slid sensually against her bare rump. She scooped her long hair out of the way of her data port and leaned forward. "I really need to tie this hair up."

Amun carefully plugged the data jack into the port at the back of her skull. "I prefer to see all those wanton fiery curls down."

Wanton fiery curls? Luxi rolled her eyes. "I noticed, but it gets tangled on everything."

Amun leaned over the desk to access the holographic keyboard display. "I'm sure you'll manage just fine." He turned and flashed a smile. "Let's see what you need."

Luxi felt the scan shimmering at the back of her thoughts.

"Ah, your array and interfacing is quite current, but you definitely need data files, including a number of languages." He tapped the top of her hand. "Incoming data."

Luxi closed her eyes and cleared her mind. It was better to simply let it go where it needed to be without bothering to scan through it. It saved on download time.

"Are you going to tell her?" Leto asked softly.

Luxi opened her eyes.

Amun had his back to her, facing Leto. "Of course."

Leto raised his brow at Amun as he tied a knee-length robe of deep silver over the black silk. "Now would be good." He picked up a black sash, and his eyes narrowed. "Before the jewelry?"

Alarm jangled along Luxi's spine. "Am I in some kind of trouble?"

"Not at all." Amun lifted his chin but did not turn to face Luxi. "You are safe from Vincent and listed on my staff as my personal secretary."

Safe from Vincent and gainfully employed, thank Glory! Luxi released a sigh. "Then Vincent's claim was false?"

Amun peered at the floor. "Not quite."

Luxi's hands tightened on the arms of the chair. "Not quite?"

"Amun . . ." Leto rolled his eyes. "Just say it."

Amun turned to face her, but his gaze was focused on the holographic display floating over his desk. "I'm afraid that to put you on my staff, I had to pull what is known as a dirty trick."

A dirty trick? Luxi's frown deepened. "What did you do?"

Amun pulled a shimmering card from his pocket and held it up. "I jumped Vincent's claim."

Luxi froze. A ripple of unease went through her. "Is that my data card?" The words came out breathless.

Amun turned to glance at her then turned away. "Yes."

"The kiss . . ." Luxi's pulse pounded in her throat. He had taken the card when he kissed her. "You put in a counter-claim. Only you had the card."

Amun nodded. "And your verbal consent."

Luxi blinked. Fate and Glory . . . Yes he did. In the garden she had formally 'consented' to his service.

Leto cleared his throat. "I had your DNA." He carefully avoided looking at her as he tied his robe.

Of course he did. They had just finished sex.

"Then I'm . . ." Luxi's breath stopped in her throat. "I'm . . ." She couldn't say it. She couldn't even think it. Her heart ached as though a fist had tightened around it. "Is it done?"

Amun held her gaze. "There were no delays in the processing."

Leto shrugged into a floor-length robe of black and steel gray. "You were done before you walked into the shower."

Luxi took a small shallow breath. This was it? This was the future she had chosen? Her new future was as an indentured employee, a legal slave? She stared down at the scarlet carpet, concentrating to access her talent and scan the lines of possibility. Her line of synchronicity was broad with few knots. Clearly, a future marked by very few decisions; a life under someone else's control. *Mother of Glory . . .* A shiver raked her.

Amun moved to her side in a whisper of rich silk. He dropped to one knee and set his warm hand over her chilled fingers. "Luxi, I had not intended for this to happen, but it was the only way to keep you out of Vincent's hands."

Luxi stared hard at Amun. "Then why did you ask for my 'consent'?" No employer asks for consent; there were too many legal connotations.

Amun dropped his chin and his cheeks flushed. "I will admit to considering it, that's why I asked, but I had already decided that it was unnecessary." He caught her gaze and his jaw tightened. "Vincent's active claim made it necessary."

Luxi bit her lip. Amun had to be telling the truth. It was too . . . unreal to be anything else.

Amun pressed her fingers and stood up. "I swear I will take very good care of you."

Luxi bit her lip and took a slow deep breath. There wasn't a whole lot she could do at this point. It was done. She was indentured. She was owned. Fate and Glory, it didn't feel real at all.

"Just so you know; you're not the only one." Leto wrapped the black velvet sash around his robes at his waist.

Huh? Luxi blinked at Leto. "You're . . ." She still couldn't say it. "You, too?"

"Yep, only with me it *was* deliberate." Leto jerked the knot on his sash tight. "One minute I'm a freelance contract assassin, and the next, Amun has legal rights to everything I own, including my person. He blindsided me."

Amun smiled tightly. "You should have been paying attention."

Leto snorted and started to pick up knives from the bed. "I was a little busy at the time—trying to keep you alive." He tucked small blades here and there into his sash.

Amun glanced over his shoulder at Leto. "And I was attempting to keep the Imperial guards from executing you on sight."

"Oh, that makes me feel so much better about being at the end of your leash." He smiled cynically at Luxi.

Amun leaned over the desk to check the data he was downloading into Luxi's mind. "You don't appear to be suffering."

Leto lowered his chin and peered from under his brows. "You trapped me with a legal loophole."

"I honestly didn't think it would work." Amun turned back to face Leto. "I assumed you had made provisions for it."

Luxi frowned up at Amun. "What did you do?"

Amun abruptly blushed and stared down at the carpet.

Leto scowled. "He claimed salvage rights."

"Salvage rights?" Luxi shook her head. "I don't see how?"

Amun sighed. "Leto is listed as a cyborg, but in actuality, he's completely non-biological. Therefore, he's technically . . ." He paused, biting his lip.

"Dead." Leto lifted a long black sheathed sword and belt from the bed. "I'm technically a fully functional corpse." He pulled the sword belt around his hips and buckled it. "He got a verbal consent out of me for something else, then broke into my ship's logs for the rest of the information he needed."

"I did not break in." Amun poked at the holographic display hovering over the glass desktop. "You voluntarily let me into your ship's system."

Leto frowned and picked up more blades from the bed. "Not that far."

Amun shrugged, but a smile played on his full lips. "Was it my fault your codes were easy to guess?"

"So it was *my* fault you trapped me?" Leto knelt to tuck a blade into the top of each boot.

"You should have been prepared for the attempt."

Leto straightened and groaned. "Arguing with you is like arguing with a bulkhead!"

Amun grinned suddenly. "This comes as a surprise?"

Luxi glanced from one to the other. The argument between Amun and Leto sounded more like practiced banter than a real argument. The sarcasm was loud and clear, but it sounded more like two very close friends bickering, not like real grievances. She felt a smile creep onto her lips. They sounded like an old married couple.

Leto rolled his eyes but couldn't quite bite back his tight smile. "For someone who is serious about the truth, Amun, you have no problems changing the rules when no one's looking."

Amun's brows lowered. "I don't need to change the rules. Most people are simply unaware of how to use them properly."

Luxi raised her brow at Amun. "You sound like a lawyer."

Amun snorted. "I'm a diplomat. We're much worse."

Leto shook his head. "He's not kidding. I've seen him in action."

Luxi tilted her head to look up at Amun. "Should I be worried?"

Amun sighed dramatically. "Oh, it's far too late to worry now." He turned and smiled down at Luxi. "And that appears to be all the files you need at the moment."

"Thank Glory . . ." Luxi leaned forward so Amun could unfasten the data jack. She only hoped that all the new information was in the proper place and she could access it when she needed it.

Amun coiled the data jack and set it on the desk. He lifted his head to look over at the door. "Ah, dinner has just arrived."

"It has?" Luxi's stomach took that moment to growl.

The main entry chime sounded out in the hall.

Amun's glanced down at her, his eyes wide, then smiled. "With perfect timing."

Luxi frowned toward the door. "How do you know who it is?"

Amun tapped his temple. "Our service has recognizably loud thoughts." He looked over at Leto. "Shall we go?"

"Thank the Maker. I'm starved!" Leto went to open the door.

Luxi stood up and tugged at her hair. "Go where?"

Amun smiled. "The informal dining room."

CHAPTER ELEVEN

A cross the hall, the informal dining room may have been small, but it certainly wasn't informal. Artistic frosted glass fixtures spilled golden light down the deep burgundy walls with the long wall directly across from the door, commanded by a huge window with a gorgeous view of space. The round table that seated six was covered in a white cloth that looked like real Terran Damask, the plates were Shido porcelain, and Luxi strongly suspected that the water tumblers were Dinarian crystal.

The food displayed in the heated silver tureens looked incredible. Luxi was pretty sure she recognized a few of the vegetables and the sliced roast floating in steaming juice smelled like it was from an actual bovine rather than processed.

Leto dropped into the chair on the right and started scooping food onto his plate.

Amun rolled his eyes, winked at Luxi, and walked around Leto to sit in the chair on Leto's right with his back to the window.

Luxi took the chair on Leto's left, facing the window, with her back to the door. She set her cloth napkin in her lap and served herself from each of the three steaming tureens.

Amun promptly started asking about her former duties at the last three companies she'd worked in.

Luxi replied as politically correct as possible. She had never found it good business to mention some of her former employer's nastier habits.

Amun then posed a pile of questions on his personal

schedule.

Luxi answered succinctly and smiled. Apparently, Amun was checking to see if the information he'd downloaded was filed properly. Then, she realized that Amun's questions had been posed in a variety of languages. *Well, damn, looks like my translator's up to speed.* She sipped at her water to cover her smile. Her translation program had worked so smoothly she hadn't noticed.

Amun smiled. "So, you finally noticed that I was testing your translation program?"

Luxi choked, just a little. *Telepathy or a good guess?*

Amun raised a brow and smiled.

Ah, telepathy. Luxi used her napkin to cover her smile. She opened her mouth to make a comment and her inner scheduling alarm went off. Amun's appointment was in ten minutes. She rose from her chair. "The negotiations appointment! We're going to be late!"

Amun set his glass down. "Ah, the ten-minute warning."

Luxi nodded.

"Good." Amun rose from his chair and smiled. He turned to Leto. "Are we ready?"

Leto set down his fork and used his napkin hastily. "Yep." He tossed the napkin onto his plate, stood up and headed for the door. "Let's go."

After collecting Luxi's heavy cream court robe from where they had left it on the bed, they left the guards standing by the suite door and strode deeper into the suite's apartments. In a small, side alcove was a lift door. Leto pressed the call button on the side and leaned back against the alcove's wall.

Luxi blinked at the blank reflective door. "You have your own private lift?"

Amun patted her shoulder. "It is standard in diplomatic suites. For far more secure arrival at conferences."

Amun and Luxi stood at the back of the lift facing the door while Leto applied a slide key to the menu panel on the door's right. He punched in a destination, nodded, then leaned back against the right wall. He focused on Luxi and his smile became decidedly lascivious.

Luxi's cheeks heated under Leto's stare. She scowled. "What?"

"I was just thinking . . ." Leto folded his arms and lifted his knee to prop one booted heel on the wall behind him. "About the panties you're not wearing."

The air exploded from Luxi's lungs. "Leto!"

Amun covered his mouth, closed his eyes briefly and inhaled deeply. "Children, this is not the time to play."

Leto raised a brow and his smile broadened. "That never stopped you."

A small smile lifted Amun's lips. "That is entirely beside the point."

The lift door opened on a hallway painted a deep gold with autumn red carpeting. An energy grid crackled before the door at the far end.

Leto stepped out of the lift.

Luxi took a shuddering breath. Just beyond that grid were the crowned heads of whole planetary systems. It was exciting. It was terrifying. Luxi froze. What was she doing here?

Amun took Luxi's chilled hand and folded it over his arm. "Relax. You are only required to sit still and be pleasant to anyone who addresses you." He drew her from the lift with a small tug.

"Sit still, be pleasant. Okay." Luxi lifted her chin and tugged her mouth into a smile. "Sounds like every other job I've had."

Amun grinned. "The display may be rather pretty, but I assure you, you will find the conference itself to be deadly dull in a matter of minutes."

Leto turned back to grin at her. "Do what I do, stare out the big window." He frowned and stopped, then turned to face them. "Amun, the jewelry?"

Amun jerked to a halt. "Oh, yes." He reached into his pocket and tugged up his robes, to kneel down on one knee. "Luxi, may I have your left foot?"

Luxi blinked. "My foot?"

Leto stepped closer and offered Luxi his hand. "You're putting it on her ankle?"

Luxi took Leto's hand for balance and lifted her slippered foot.

Amun took her foot in his hand and enclosed a plain iridescent ring around her ankle. "No need to announce her status."

Luxi's heart thumped in her chest. It was a binding ring, meant to control the wearer by tapping into their internal robotics, their augmentations. They were worn by indentured staff to keep track of their whereabouts and actions. She looked up at Leto.

Leto peeled back his left sleeve to show her a similar ring. He smiled and shrugged.

She frowned. He hadn't been wearing it earlier.

Amun released her foot. "There, that will take care of security's concerns."

Luxi felt a shiver in her mind and the hair lifted at the back of her neck. The ring was tapping into her internal computational.

Amun stood. "It's only temporary. Security demands that all indentured staff wear them during conferences. I'll take it off when we return to the suite." He leaned close to her ear. "I know you're not an assassin." He turned to smile at Leto.

Leto's smile soured. "Very funny." He turned and headed for the sizzling grid. The grid snapped off to let him pass, then snapped right back on. He turned around. "Come on you two."

Luxi stopped before the grid and swallowed. That thing could kill her in seconds.

"Your clearance is already programmed." Amun pushed Luxi gently after Leto.

The grid snapped off.

Luxi lunged through the grid and plowed straight into Leto's arms.

Leto grinned down at her. "Scared?"

Luxi stepped out of Leto's arms and her cheeks heated ferociously. "Who, me?" She stepped to the side.

Amun proceed through the grid at a far more sedate pace with an amused smile. "Luxi, you shouldn't torment Leto like that."

Luxi sucked in a breath. "Torment *him*?"

Amun shrugged as he stepped between them. "For goodness sake, woman . . ." He smiled slyly. "You aren't even wearing panties." He pressed his palm on a lighted grid by the door.

Luxi's mouth fell open and her temper surged in a nice refreshing rush. "And whose idea was that?"

Amun raised his brows and his smile broadened to a grin. "Why, mine, of course."

The door opened — onto sedate pandemonium.

The assembly hall was completely circular and smaller than Luxi had expected it to be with triple tiered amphitheater seating. The curving walls were a soft gold and riddled with doors framed by frosted glass light fixtures — and uniformed security guards.

The pair of guards by their door each held up a hand-held computational. They scanned their readings, shared a glance and nodded at Amun.

Amun proceeded down the shallow steps with Luxi and Leto behind him.

Luxi looked up, and up . . . The ceiling was a clear dome with an incredible view of the pink, orange and green swirls of the nearby nebula.

Leto stepped closer. "Great view huh?"

Luxi had to remember to breathe. "Wow."

Amun glanced back at them. "Leto used that very word, the first time he saw it, too."

Leto scowled. "Did not."

Amun lifted a brow and grinned as he continued down the steps. "Did so."

At the lowest level, a long black glass table occupied the very center of the assembly hall with twelve chairs. A number of diplomats from assorted races in jewel-toned court robes circulated around the table. Even more robed people of many races and descriptions milled and chatted in the auditorium seats surrounding the center.

Amun was hailed by an older gentleman with a long white braid in midnight blue robes. He approached with a smile and bowed. Light gleamed on the iridescent circlet he wore. He was an Imperial Lord.

Amun bowed. "Senator Shodu . . ."

Leto caught Luxi's hand. "Take a seat in the first row. We'll come get you when we're done."

Luxi caught at Leto's sleeve. "Where are you going to be?"

Leto smiled. "Amun gets to sit in one of the big chairs, I get to stand behind him and be menacing."

Luxi raised a brow at him. "Menacing huh?" She smiled. *Right* . . ."Sure you can do that?"

Leto lifted his chin and stared down his long nose. "Is that a challenge?" His smile sharpened and shadows moved in the depth of his eyes.

Luxi shivered in spite of herself.

Leto nodded. "I thought not." He turned and strode after Amun.

Luxi sighed and sat in the red velvet fold-down seat by the aisle. "Pest."

Leto turned back. "I heard that!"

Luxi grinned. "Good!"

Amun lifted his head from his conversation to look at Luxi and then Leto sternly.

Leto's expression was a study in innocence as he took up a position a step away from Amun's right shoulder.

The Senator Shodu gestured toward the table and Amun moved toward one of the chairs close to the middle.

"It *is* you! I thought I recognized that hair."

Luxi turned.

Bel, the violet-eyed lord from the tram smiled at her as he stepped down the aisle. His pale cream mane was pulled back into a loose tail that fell over the shoulder of his rich gold robes. A lord's circlet graced his pale brow. "Well hello."

His two dark-eyed fems, Orah and Faro, dressed in sleek black skinsuits grinned from either side. Their slender hands rested comfortably on their hip-slung sword-belts.

Luxi sucked in a sharp breath. *Fate and glory, he* would *show up here!* She hastily rose from her seat and bowed. "Honored lord."

He gave her a formal nod and his full lips curved in a delicate smirk. "So that reprobate cyborg still has you, does he?"

Luxi winced.

Bel blinked and gave her a blinding smile. "Oh dear, your translator is working properly."

Luxi bit her lip. "I had an upgrade."

Bel laughed and his cheeks flushed pink. "Please accept my apologies for my rudeness."

Luxi raised her brow and the corner of her lips lifted in half a smile. "I'll do my best."

Bel's brows shot up and his cheeks flushed. "Oh, fatal strike . . ."

Amun arrived at Luxi's side in a rustle of silk. "Lord Belauros." He nodded and smiled. "Are you propositioning one of my employees again?"

Leto winked at Luxi from behind Amun's right shoulder.

Bel chuckled softly. "Lord Amun." He nodded toward Leto. "I'm afraid that I find both of your lovely employees a difficult temptation to resist." He raised a pale brow. "I'd be more than happy to negotiate a trade agreement; my two for your two for an evening?"

Both fems nodded vigorously, grinning broadly.

Amun lifted his chin and glanced up at the nebula-filled ceiling. "That is a very enticing offer. However, I have yet to fully explore the . . . range of my employees' skills." He smiled at Bel then his gaze drifted to Luxi. "Especially that of my newest."

Luxi's cheeks heated under Amun's heavy-lidded and smoldering stare.

"From what I've seen so far . . ." Bel flashed a smile at Luxi. "I understand perfectly why you would not be ready to . . . share."

Heat filled Luxi's cheeks as a visceral memory of the tram ride with Bel watching her and Leto avidly burned through her. She bit her lip and looked away.

Bel chuckled and moved down the steps to Amun's side. "I would also be more than interested in discussing some of *your* more esoteric talents. Perhaps privately, over coffee?"

Amun sighed. "Bel, you are incorrigible." He turned toward the gathering of lords.

Bel nodded and aimed his spectacular smile at Amun. "I do try."

"You succeed." Amun walked away, leading Bel and his fems toward the broad table. "But coffee does sound nice . . ."

Leto turned back to Luxi. "Be good," he said in a loud stage whisper, then turned and fell in behind Amun.

Luxi's mouth fell open. *Me?* She rolled her eyes and sat down. All around her, other robed members began taking seats in the amphitheater.

At the main negotiation table, Lord Bel took a seat on one end of the table with the senator occupying the other end and Amun taking a chair in the center. Various other lords seated themselves around them, leaving the chair opposite Amun empty.

Luxi was surprised and pleased to discover that she could hear everything they were saying perfectly.

It seemed that Senator Shodu represented the governing republic of one world and Lord Belauros represented the royal house of another. They were discussing the disposition of a pair of colony worlds that wished to open trade, but a third world was pirating the trade routes between them. Representatives from neighboring worlds, also interested in the negotiations were seated around the table. The representative of the third world in question had yet to appear.

According to what Luxi was overhearing, the third world was not pleased to have a professional telepath as part of the negotiation. Unfortunately, neither the senator nor Lord Bel would hold the conference without Amun to monitor the honesty of the representatives.

Luxi looked up at the brilliant nebula filling the dome overhead and felt her talent stir. Synchronicity was shifting, hard and fast. She opened her mind to her talent and reeled under a lashing hurricane of far-reaching changes that affected everyone in the room. Threads snarled and snapped with world-heavy consequences.

Beneath it, her other smaller talent began to stir. The talent that sensed the dead.

Too occupied to worry about ghosts, Luxi gripped the chair's arms and strained to ride the cresting temporal wave of shifting potential futures. If she could find the center of the storm, the fulcrum point, she could figure out what triggered this mess and perhaps sound a warning . . .

At the table, Amun stood, staring hard at Luxi.

Luxi caught the movement and her talent seized on him. Amun was the center of the storm. Something was about to happen to him—something fatal.

From a side aisle, a massive man in an exquisitely formal, ship captain's floor-length frock coat in deep scarlet came striding down the steps. Two well-armed cyborgs in ship's livery strode at his heels.

They were the other half of the storm. They were going to kill Amun.

Luxi lunged out of her chair. *Amun!*

Amun held up his hand and shook his head. He turned to Leto and whispered.

Luxi stood before her chair, shaking with the urgency of her vision.

Leto nodded and his gaze narrowed on the approaching trio.

Amun smiled, nodded toward Luxi and rose from his chair. Calmly, he moved to a new seat, one closer to the senator and further from the empty seats in the middle.

Luxi bit her lip. Amun had picked up her frantic warning. *Thank the Maker.* But the storm of change had not quite died down. Something was still going to happen. It wasn't over yet.

CHAPTER TWELVE

The scarlet-coated ship's captain stepped up onto the dais where the representatives were gathered. His two cyborgs stopped at the bottom step directly behind him.

Lord Bel and Senator Shodu exchanged glances and rose from their chairs.

Lord Bel smiled. "I'm glad you could join us, Captain Faraday."

Captain Faraday folded his arms across his chest and lifted his chin. "I protest negotiating with a telepath present."

Senator Shodu smiled. "We understand and accept. However, negotiations will not proceed without one."

Luxi felt the lines of synchronicity shiver with tension. A decision was being made.

Captain Faraday looked around the table at the seated representatives.

Luxi bit her lip. *He's looking for the telepath. He's looking for Amun.*

Both Lord Bel and the senator remained focused on the captain.

Lord Bel smiled. "With all due respect, would you kindly leave your exceedingly well-armed companions off the floor?"

Captain Faraday scowled. "Why? You have your guards."

Lord Bel's smile broadened. "Yes, but as you can see, they are far from marine-augmented."

Captain Faraday jerked his head toward his guards. They saluted and stepped back.

Bel lifted his hand toward the table. "Thank you. We will begin as soon as you are ready."

Captain Faraday strode around the table and took Amun's vacated chair at the back.

A shimmer of energy flashed around the dais. An energy grid had been activated. The negotiation table was sealed from all entry or exit. Captain Faraday's cyborgs would not be able to step up onto the dais.

Luxi swallowed. Nor would anyone else.

Captain Faraday scowled.

Senator Shodu smiled. "A precaution against assassinations. You never know who is seated in the audience." He waved his hand to indicate the dozens of people seated in the amphitheater.

A light wave of soft laughter erupted from said audience.

Lord Bel and Senator Shodu glanced at Amun who pretended not to notice.

Captain Faraday caught the glance and focused on Amun.

Luxi's talent howled as the synchronistic tension broke. Captain Faraday had identified Amun as the telepath.

Amun stared straight at the captain and smiled, no longer bothering to hide. At his shoulder, Leto smiled as well and succeeded in appearing thoroughly menacing.

Bel lifted a glass to catch the captain's attention. "When you are ready, Captain Faraday."

The captain nodded and sighed as he slowly stood.

Luxi's talent screamed in warning.

Amun glanced at Luxi.

Captain Faraday flicked a knife toward Amun's heart.

Leto leaned over and caught the blade in his outstretched hand. He grinned at the captain. "Nice try."

Captain Faraday hissed. "Belmortus?"

Leto's eyes narrowed, and he smiled. "That's me."

Amun smiled thinly. "My personal bodyguard is known

for his short temper. I would not try that again."

Captain Faraday clenched his jaw. "Then I won't." He vaulted onto the table toward Amun in a blur of speed, drawing his sword and dagger.

Leto launched onto the tabletop to meet him. His serrated daggers caught the captain's descending sword and turned the blade. He slashed for the captain's throat . . .

The entire table erupted with furious bodyguards lunging onto the table to join the fight. Papers scattered, delegates scattered, the gathered audience screamed. The captain's two heavily armored cyborgs shouted, hovering at the edges of the energy field with their blades drawn.

The guards posted at the lift doors charged down the aisles with their swords drawn. The captain's marine cyborgs turned to engage them with serrated daggers nearly as long at the guard's swords.

Two guards rushed past Luxi.

And an arm closed tight around Luxi's throat.

Luxi grabbed onto the choking arm, tugging at the sleeve, and was hauled backwards out of her chair. Her mind battered by the whirling potentials she barely felt the under-hum of her other talent.

Leto pinned Captain Faraday face down on the table and set the point of his serrated dagger at the base of the captain's skull. "Move and die."

Faro, Bel's fem, slapped restraints on the captain's wrists.

Luxi gasped for breath and felt the potentials shift — but not change. Amun was still in danger.

Leto lifted his head and spotted Luxi being dragged backwards up the stairs. He leapt off the table. "Shut down the grid!"

No, you idiot! Sucking for air, Luxi screamed. "No! It's not done yet!" She twisted against her captor and dug in her heels. "Amun . . ." She gasped as the arm jerked her off her feet. She stumbled backwards. "Save Amun!"

Amun joined Leto at the grid's barrier. At their feet, the guards and the marines were knotted in a vicious battle. Blood sprayed and hissed against the grid.

Amun lifted his head. "Shut down the grid!"

"No! Don't!" Her shouts were cut off by the arm around her throat. *Stupid men!* She wasn't in deadly danger—Amun was! Actually, she wasn't sure. Amun's fate was so huge, she couldn't even sense hers. But, for goodness sake, she was only a secretary. The fate of whole worlds rested in Amun's survival. She didn't actually matter . . . to anybody.

Tears stung her eyes. Fate, she hated crying. She yanked at the arm that held her. She had to warn them, and this moron was interfering with her *job*! Temper flared and she dug in her heels. "Let go!" She twisted hard around to face her choker and shouted. "I'm busy!"

Her attacker caught her by the wrists. His face was exotic in shape with pin-straight short-cropped black hair. His almond-shaped eyes were filled with moving darkness. He smiled. "What a terrible shame." His voice was a frigid wind that sliced through her mind. "I'm afraid you simply must come with me."

What? Luxi shivered as her second talent surged within her. *Another man with a ghost?* She blinked at him, he looked . . . odd.

The man wore a plain high-collared uniform of gray-green with brass buttons and scarlet trim. A short cape lined in scarlet satin fell from his shoulders to the broad red sash knotted around his waist. A plain sheathed sword and an equally plain sheathed knife as long as her forearm was shoved in his sash by his hip. His knee-high booted feet rested a full inch above the floor.

Great Glory! He didn't have a ghost—he *was* a ghost. Ice water flooded her veins. She shoved back frantically. "No!"

The ghost twisted her arms brutally behind her, swinging her around to face the lift door at the top of the stairs. "Yes."

Luxi gasped at the pain in her elbows and shoulders, never mind her wrists. *Fate, this ghost is strong!* Her arms were close to being dislocated.

"Go." He shoved her forward and up the stairs at nearly a trot.

Luxi winced as her toes slammed into the steps before she could lift her feet. "Why are you doing this?"

"You have an appointment."

"An appointment with who?"

The ghost shoved her tight up against the silver lift door. He pulled her right arm from her back and slammed her palm against the call box. "With Vincent, my host."

"Vincent?" *Oh, shit!* She was in the hands of Vincent's ghost. Temper and terror slammed through Luxi in a potent mix. "Oh, hell no I don't!" She bucked in his hold, furious and horrified. "I don't associate with assholes!"

The lift doors opened.

"How impolite." He shoved her into the lift.

Luxi didn't quite slam against the wall and whirled around. "I am not going anywhere with you!" She charged for the open door.

The ghost caught her around the waist and practically threw her bodily toward the back of the lift. "Yes, you are."

That time Luxi did slam into the wall. She barely missed knocking her head, but she still had to gasp for breath.

The lift doors closed.

Luxi lunged for the closed door. It was not going to open. She didn't have the slide key to activate it. "Damnit!" She turned to face the ghost. "You can't do this!"

"It is done." The ghost smiled and walked toward her.

Luxi scooted back and away from him. "I don't have a key. I can't activate the lift."

"No need for a key." Bypassing Luxi completely, the ghost plunged his hand into the menu panel on the door's right without damaging it in any way. "Electronics respond well to me." The panel activated and the lift began to proceed. "There, no need for concern."

Luxi swallowed. *No need for concern? Yeah right!* To everyone and everything, the ghost was exactly that—a ghost. Except to those with Luxi's strange little talent. To her, the ghost was as solid as flesh and blood. And dangerous. Those phantom blades on his hip would pass through any normal person with leaving only a cold shiver behind, but they were as deadly to her as true steel.

She knotted her hands into fists. "But I don't belong to Vincent!"

The ghost's smile broadened. "Vincent? You're not for him. You're for me. He's simply going to provide for your care."

Luxi's mouth fell open. "You? What for?"

"Those of your kind, feed my kind." The ghost's eyes narrowed. "Vincent is my host, but there is not enough in him on which to dine properly. On you, I shall feed well."

Feed? Luxi shook with rage. Anger was good. Anger kept the fear away. She bared her teeth at him. "Over my dead body!"

"If need be." The ghost chuckled. "But I doubt it will be necessary." He pulled his hand from the control panel.

The lift stopped and the lighting flickered. They were between floors.

The ghost unfastened his cape and dropped it. The cape fluttered briefly then disappeared altogether. He reached up to tug on the red satin tasseled cord held through his scarlet epaulet. The waist-draping loops passed under and around his right shoulder about three times. Pulled completely free it looked about four feet long. He focused tightly on Luxi and wrapped one end of the slender satin cord loosely around his wrist, letting the other end dangle, floating around him like a serpent.

Luxi eyed the phantom rope and backed up against the opposite wall. She clenched her jaw. "I am not going to let you tie my hands."

The ghost tilted his head and snorted. "Dear child, this is not for your hands. Remove the robe."

"What?" Luxi choked. "No!"

The ghost pursed his lips and shrugged. "I can choke you to barely conscious and do this with you on the floor, right through your clothes. To me, only your skin is substantial. Or you can stay upright and awake." His smile returned. "I prefer your cooperation. Choking leaves such nasty bruises on the throat."

Luxi bit her lip. If he choked her unconscious, there was no telling what *else* he'd do. "Just the robe?"

"I need to see what you have under it."

Luxi snorted. "You could have asked! I have a dress on."

"How long?"

Luxi frowned. "To the floor."

"Ah." He nodded. "Then you will need to raise your skirts to above your waist."

Raise her skirts? Luxi reeled back against the wall. "Oh, hell no! Forget it!"

The ghost shrugged. "Very well, choking it is." He took two long steps toward her and raised his hands.

Luxi slid and then rolled away from him, but there wasn't any place to go in a lift. His hand caught in her hair. She jerked to a halt. "Ow! Shit!"

He caught her shoulder and spun her around to face him.

Luxi screamed and scratched for his eyes.

He sneered and turned his head away from her clawing fingers, then shoved her with the flat of his hand against her breastbone, slamming her breathless against the wall. His hands closed around her throat high up, his thumbs pressing deep into the pulses under her jaw.

Luxi couldn't breathe, not in, not out, and her head was getting light fast. She dug her fingers into his hands.

"One last chance. Cooperate or go to sleep. If we do it this way you will awaken with a vicious headache, that is if I don't squeeze too hard and kill you accidentally." His hands loosened.

Luxi gasped for breath and her pulse slammed in her ears. She glared up at him.

He raised his brow.

She held his stare, trying desperately not to give in to the fear howling for her attention. "Fine. I'll do it."

He backed away and smiled. "I am pleased."

CHAPTER THIRTEEN

Luxi turned away from the archaically uniformed ghost and unfastened her cream and gold court robe and let the heavy silk slide from her arms.

The ghost tugged the robe from her fingers and tossed it to the far corner of the lift.

Luxi scowled and bent over to part the bottom half of her pale cream robe and the white silk robe beneath it, then grabbed the sheer shift.

"All of it."

Luxi lifted her head. "All of what?"

The ghost leaned back against the wall with his arms folded. "Lift *all* of your clothing and remove your undergarments."

Luxi froze. She wasn't wearing undergarments, Amun's idea, of course. The brief flash of annoyance brought back what little was left of her courage. She took in a deep breath, released it, grabbed everything and lifted. She was standing against the wall with her crotch exposed. It was humiliating. Her cheeks filled with heat and she turned away, closing her eyes.

"No undergarments, and yet, you blush. How interesting."

Luxi's eyes snapped open. He was kneeling right in front of her, looking up at her with his brow raised. She hadn't heard him move. She rolled her eyes. Of course she hadn't heard him move. *He's a ghost.* They didn't actually make sounds.

He snorted, and lowered his gaze, focusing on her crotch.

He reached up and caught her above the knees. "Wider. Stand wider."

Luxi shivered under his cool fingers and parted her legs.

He uncoiled the cord from his wrist and carefully folded the entire length in half. The twisted satin cord looked a lot longer this close and about as slender as her finger.

Luxi frowned. "What are you going to do with that?"

He glanced up and a smile lifted the corner of his mouth. "Bind you." He leaned forward and passed the folded cord behind her, bringing it up to her waist, then took the tasseled ends and passed them through the loop at the other end. He brought the loose ends up, then passed them down, under the double cord around her waist, against her skin, then through the resulting loop at the bottom, and pulled the knot snug. His fingers tugged at the cords binding her waist, loosening it just a bit.

Luxi didn't get it. The cords weren't even tight around her. "You're tying my waist?"

"No." He leaned back, keeping hold of the cords' ends. "Turn around."

Luxi turned around, totally confused.

The ghost brought his hands around and passed the cords between her legs. "I am binding your cunt." He slid the ends under the cords around her waist and pulled it.

Luxi gasped. The cords slid up between the plump outer lips of her pussy to press against her clit and continued back and up the division of her ass cheeks to the cords around her waist. "But why?"

The ghost tugged the cords snug, but not tight. "I need your climax to feed." He slid two fingers along the snug cords, brushing her intimately.

She shivered in sheer revulsion. "What has that got to do with a rope?"

He set two fingers right over her clit. "The binding will

stimulate a swift rise so that you will be ready for swift release when I take you." Holding that one spot between his fingertips, he tugged the cords free. "Turn back around, slowly."

Luxi turned around and stared down at the top of the ghost's head. She seriously doubted anything would get her hot enough to enjoy anything he did to her. "You're going to rape me." It wasn't a question.

"Yes." The ghost made a knot where his fingers marked. "I feed on pleasure, terror, or death." He looked up at her. "Which would you prefer?"

Luxi turned away and bit her lip. *I'd prefer to be home and asleep.* But home was gone. She took a shaky breath. *I don't think Leto and Amun are going to get me out of this one.* She closed her eyes. *As long as I'm breathing, there's a way out. I just have to be ready for the opportunity when it comes.*

The ghost made a second knot about three inches further down. "Death delivers the entire essence all at once, but of course, the servant is no more. Death is wasteful in one with gifts as plentiful as yours." He set his hands on her thighs. "Turn back around."

Luxi turned around and stared at the wall. *At least I'm more valuable alive than dead.*

The ghost brought the cords to the front and passed it between her legs. "Terror delivers a scanty amount and tends to render the servant incapable of functioning independently. It eventually destroys the mind." He pushed the tasseled ends up under the cords knotted around her waist. "Pleasure's release gives the largest essence without destroying the servant's mind, or the servant."

Luxi hunched her shoulders, chilled. It was like he was reciting a menu or something.

"However, inducing pleasure in a reluctant servant curbs the will." He drew the cord snug. "Your will could benefit from curbing. You will live longer." He tugged.

Luxi's head came up and she inhaled sharply. The small

knot put pressure right on top of her clit and the other knot pressured the sensitive spot just beyond her body's entrance, just under her anus.

The ghost slid his fingers down along the cords and under, parting her intimate curls and pressing on each of the knots.

Luxi bit her lips as her clit pulsed in confused interest. She shivered and the hair stood on the back of her neck.

He chuckled softly. "Perfect placement." He slid both his hands under her and gently finger-tugged the cords apart, framing her clit between them then pressing the twin cords between her tender folds. "By the time we arrive, you will be more than ready for me."

Luxi closed her eyes tight and bit back her humiliated moan. *Glory, what a sadistic asshole!*

"When I thrust into you between the cords, I will be squeezed as though you were a virgin." He slid a finger under the cords at her tailbone, loosened it a touch and knotted the ends swiftly. "And you are bound." He stepped back. "Very nice." He sighed. "Too bad there really isn't time for other pleasures. You may drop your skirts."

Luxi hastily dropped her skirts. She had no interest in what the ghost considered 'other pleasures.'

The ghost strode back to the lift's panel and thrust his hand in.

The lights flickered and the lift proceeded.

Luxi bent over to tug the under-robe and shift back into order. The cords and knots shifted against her clit, drawing forth a warm curl of interest. She froze. It felt as though a pair of fingers gently squeezed her clit and rubbed it at the same time. Her nipples tingled in reaction. *Oh shit, the stupid thing actually works!*

She had to take a breath before she could continue. If this idea had belonged to anyone other than the ghost, she might have found the binding entertaining . . . but there was nothing entertaining about the fate he had planned for her. *Rape and draining . . .*

Fate! There has to be a way out of this! Keeping her back to him, she straightened slowly and opened to her talent for viewing the possibilities. Strands of synchronicity and decision stretched within her mind's eye.

"What are you doing?"

Luxi froze. He could sense that? She took a breath and scanned down her lines as fast as she could. "I'm contemplating my future." It was the absolute truth.

He chuckled. "Your future will be long if you are obedient."

Luxi looked at the lift wall but focused on her talent. The strands showed her a juncture, a decision that shifted away from the ghost and Vincent's future. *Good.* She led her talent fall back to a soft hum that would let her know when it was time, but no more.

It was all a matter of waiting for that opportunity to arrive. She just hoped she spotted the turning point in enough time to use it. She also hoped nothing happened to close that opportunity off. Too many strands of decision and potential surrounded it. One wrong move and that option would dissolve.

That meant continuing exactly as she had been, antagonistic, but not too much. She did not want him to choke her unconscious or pull out those phantom blades. She needed to upright and whole to make a good escape. It was a delicate balance. She didn't want the ghost to think she had any hope left. But she didn't want him to think she'd given in entirely either.

She pulled back her foot and kicked, striking the wall with the ball of her foot. The impact made a nice satisfying metallic bang. She released a breath. It didn't do any good whatsoever, but it made her feel a whole lot better.

The ghost laughed.

Within her, a strand of possibility pulled away and dissolved, strengthening her path toward escape.

"Come here." The ghost's voice was chill and commanding.

Warily, Luxi approached.

"Do not fight and all will be well." He slid his hand under her hair and caught a handful at the base of her neck. He tugged for good measure.

Luxi winced. *Asshole.*

"Remember, no one can see me, but you. Walk slowly and do not look into anyone's face." He pulled his hand from the lift panel.

The lift stopped

Luxi glanced toward the pile of cream silk in the corner. "My robe!"

"No."

The doors opened onto a dark hallway.

"Go."

Luxi stepped out into darkness.

A hum echoed around her and lights flickered into being around them, revealing a disused and filthy cross hallway. To the left and to the right, the hallway continued in darkness. The walls were plain steel painted with broad bands of metallic brown. They were somewhere in the Bronze district.

Luxi trembled. No one would even think to look down here for her.

The ghost turned her toward the left. "Walk."

Luxi walked. The ghost fell into step with her, his fingers snug in her hair, but not pinching. Around them, the lights bloomed into being, only to shut down as they passed. "Are you doing that, with the lights?"

"Yes." He snorted. "I do not need light, but I have no desire to have you fall and harm yourself."

"Oh." If she wanted to go back to the lift, it would be a run in the dark—chased by a ghost that didn't need light to see. Not a good plan. Her hands bunched the sides of her robe.

"Where are you taking me?"

"Someplace secure."

Luxi grimaced. That answer was *so* not helpful. She took a steadying breath. *Okay, what's down here on Bronze?* The lower income housing and cheap motels were supposed to be in Bronze. She was pretty sure she remembered reading about some kind of shopping district, too, so sooner or later, they would come to a populated area . . .

Her talent shimmered within her. Luxi bit her lip to hide her smile. That was where her chance of escape was, somewhere in a populated area. Her best guess was the shopping district. Was there anything else down here? Yes, as a matter of fact; direct access to privately docked ships.

A shimmer of possibility moved through her. A ship *was* woven into her possible future, the one she was trying to avoid. That had to be where the ghost was taking her. A shudder of alarm shook her. If she got on that ship, all futures closed to one dark thread.

"Is something wrong?"

"Wrong?" A spurt of sour humor startled a choked laugh out of Luxi. "You mean besides the fact that I'm the prisoner of a sadistic ghost that's going to rape me?"

The ghost snorted. "By the time we reach our destination, it will not be rape."

Luxi ground her teeth. "Yeah, right."

A nasty chuckle echoed along her outer thoughts. "Tell me how do you find wearing the binding?"

Luxi had been focusing on other issues for a reason; to get her mind off the knots pressing and rubbing intimately with every single step. But now *he* wanted to talk about it. She took a careful breath. "It doesn't hurt."

"This binding is not designed to be painful, merely stimulating."

Luxi bit her lip. Now that her attention was on the cords

rubbing back and forth against her clit, it was hard to ignore that she was definitely feeling stimulated. The cords were getting damp, too. Her clit gave an interested throb. *Change the subject! Change the subject! Change the subject!* "Um, there are painful ones?" She winced. Not a good change in subjects.

"A great many." He chuckled. "Are you getting wet?"

"Uh . . ."

"It is a simple matter for me to check . . ."

Fate no, she didn't want him to check! "Yes." *Damnit.*

"Good."

Piss . . . Luxi scowled and ground her teeth as she walked.

The lights flickered on directly ahead, revealing a heavy steel circular blast door. They had come to the end of the hall.

Luxi stared up at the door. "I can't open that."

"I can." The ghost tugged her close to the right wall. He plunged his hand within and rummaged. "Ah!"

A ringing grinding noise filled the small hallway. The door screeched in protest and rolled very slowly to the left. A siren wail blasted into the hall.

Luxi winced. *Looks like somebody noticed that the door was open.*

The ghost shoved her through the widening crack and into screaming pandemonium.

CHAPTER FOURTEEN

Luxi's first impressions were big, dark, noisy, and crowded. They had come out in the middle of a busy, multilevel shopping bazaar choked with tossed-together stalls made of every conceivable material. The light was uncertain and came from a million different directions, none of which were overhead. Bodies, human and otherwise, mostly otherwise, jostled her as they fought to either get *to* the opening door, or *from* it, and everyone was shouting.

Shoved among the throng by the ghost, Luxi tripped a lot. The floors were painfully uneven with cables strewn across them. The smell of oil and aging steel was overpowering. So was the smell of too many bodies of too many descriptions. Alarms were shrieking everywhere.

Luxi flinched under the noise, then stilled. Alarms meant security was coming. Her talent shimmered with tension. It was time to escape.

Luxi let the ghost propel her forward and allowed herself to be jostled back and forth by the anxious crowd.

The ghost's hands tightened in her hair and swore viciously as he fought to hang onto her.

It was coming; the opportunity was coming . . .

Luxi felt a hard shove and found herself in the direct path of a rather large and fast-moving bi-pedal saurian. This was it. She froze and braced for impact.

The saurian slammed into her with incredible force, knocking her spinning and breathless out of his path. Luxi's hair ripped as she was torn right out of the ghost's grasp, then over and into someone's item-filled stall.

Luxi bit back a moan and opened her eyes. She had rolled into a huge pile of mechanical odds and ends she couldn't begin to identify, and they had spilled everywhere. She shifted among the pile. Everything had corners and they were digging into every inconvenient place on her body. There were going to be some nasty bruises all over her tomorrow.

Someone was shouting obscenities very close by.

She looked up.

The bright-blue humanoid shop owner was screaming at the massive saurian — and the saurian was barking right back.

She sucked in a breath. *Time to go!* Luxi ducked her head and rolled cautiously out from under the pile. She pulled up her skirts and crawled on her hands and knees, to the open back of the shop. There wasn't much room to maneuver; the shop was right up against a steel wall. As soon as both aliens were out of view, she got up on her feet and bolted along the steel wall, scooting behind the backs of dozens of makeshift stalls. *Got to find security!*

The uneven floor and deep shadows were not at all easy to negotiate at a run. There was stuff all over the floor and her slippers just weren't up to the task. Her feet were bruised in minutes. *That's it! Boots from now on!*

Running on instinct alone, she slipped between precarious booths, ducked under narrow walkways, and darted into half-lit alleys choked with people of every kind. Her talent told her that she was on the right path, but she had no idea where that path was leading. Her talent shifted in her like whiplash.

She jolted to the side, away from the oncoming . . . whatever it was, and rammed her shoulder against a pair of men in dark power armor. She yelped and fell.

They caught her elbows before her knees could hit the deck plates. "Whoa, take it easy!"

Luxi looked up in fright and prepared to run. Sojourn Corp gleamed on their breast badges. She had found security. She sagged in their hands. "Thank the maker!"

One of them shoved up his visor showing startled brown eyes. "Hey, it's that missing diplomat!"

Luxi blinked. They had been looking for her? *Wow* . . . She gave them a smile then darted a look around. Her talent was still shifting, the possibilities were still moving. She needed to get out of here. "My kidnapper is not far away. Can we go? Like right now?"

The man grinned. "Everything will be fine now, we have you."

Luxi smiled. "Thank you, but can we go?" She shoved at his armored side.

"Sure, we can go." The men laughed and set her between them. With a heavy armored hand on each shoulder, they guided her through the heart of the bazaar.

One of the guards chatted code into his helmet communicator. He looked down. "Okay, your people are coming to meet you."

Luxi blinked. *My people?* It took her an entire breath, and then it hit her. Leto and Amun were coming. They were her people. She had to blink back sudden tears. She'd never had *people* before. She'd had companies and employers and supervisors, but not people, as in, someone she mattered to.

"Hey, do you know who opened that big power door?"

The other guard snorted. "Like, she's gonna know?"

Luxi wiped at her damp cheeks. Fate and glory her hands were filthy . . ."My kidnapper did it."

"What?"

Luxi bit her lip and lengthened her stride to get them to walk faster. "The lift from the assembly hall took us to the hallway on the other side of the door. He opened the door, that's how I'm here."

"How did he open it? Only the station master has those codes."

Luxi shook her head. "You wouldn't believe me if I told you."

"Try us."

Luxi looked around. "I will, as soon as we get someplace safe."

The guards turned a sharp corner to the left, and a lift opened up right in front of her, not two steps away.

Leto, tall, dark, and very menacing, and Amun, still in his deep silver court robes, came out of the lift surrounded by four Sojourn security guards in full armor. Their mouths were tight, and they looked positively furious.

Leto and Amun stopped, staring.

Luxi stopped, unsure what to do.

Amun lunged forward and wrapped her in a tight hug. "Thank the maker!"

Leto looked around vibrating with tension. He held out his arm and herded everyone back. "Get back in. It's coming."

Amun turned sweeping Luxi before him and into the lift.

The lift doors closed.

Amun, Luxi, and Leto made a small knot in the back corner. Amun caught Luxi's shoulders. "Blood and Fate, you are *filthy!*"

Luxi flinched. "I had to do some crawling. I'm really sorry about the silk."

Amun smiled. "Clothing is replaceable; you are not. I'm simply glad you are all in one piece."

Not replaceable? Luxi stilled in shock. No one had ever said that to her before. She turned her head and blinked. Fate, what was with her, crying over every stupid little thing? She grabbed her elbows and took a deep breath. *Later, I'll think about it later.* She looked up at Amun. "How did you get down there so fast?"

Amun smiled. "We were already on the way."

Leto grinned. "Your ankle bracelet has a transmitter in it. We were tracking you the whole time."

Oddly she felt both reassured and annoyed. They could have told her . . . or had they and she'd forgotten? *I'll think about it later . . .* Luxi bit her lip. "I think he was taking me to a ship."

Amun looked over at Leto. "I suspected as much."

Leto wrapped his arm around her shoulders and grinned. "Yeah, but we have you now."

Luxi smiled at Leto. He was warm, solid, and smelled wonderful. Her core gave a hungry throb, and then another. She still had that rope thing on, and it was doing its job a little too well. Her thighs were wet with aggravated excitement. The guards were the only thing keeping her from begging one of them to press her up against the wall. She took a deep breath. *Think about something else!* "What happened with the captain that attacked you? Did they arrest him?"

Amun sighed. "He was not taken into custody."

Luxi sucked in a sharp breath. "What? Why not?"

Leto snorted. "Diplomatic immunity."

Amun sighed. "But he has been escorted off the station, and to the jump-gate."

Luxi released a breath. "I was so worried."

"You?" Leto grabbed her shoulders and turned her to face him. "When I saw that ghost drag you off, I about leaped through the grid!"

Amun cleared his throat. "Being crisped beyond redemption would not have done anyone much good."

Leto scowled. "Not all of me is physical."

Amun set his hand on Leto's shoulder. "But some of your more interesting parts are. I'd prefer if you kept them intact." He smiled. "For me." He turned to Luxi. "However did you get away?"

Luxi grinned. "I followed my talent. There was a loophole in the possibilities, so I took it."

"Good girl." Leto looked over at Amun and clenched his jaw. "We really need to deal with Vincent . . ."

Luxi shook her head. "It's not Vincent we need to worry about . . .

Amun frowned. "No?"

Luxi's hands tightened on her elbows. "I think the ghost is really in charge."

Amun nodded. "I thought that might be the case." He turned to Leto. "We *do* need a specialist . . ."

The lights flickered.

Luxi looked up and shivered hard. "It's the ghost. He's going to stop the lift."

Amun turned to Leto and caught his wrist. "Whatever happens, do not leave her side."

Leto scowled. "Why? Where are you going?"

"To collect our specialist." Amun smiled. "Unless you'd rather I stayed with Luxi . . ."

"No." Leto scowled. "Get that specialist and get back fast — and take the damned guards with you!"

"I intend to." Amun's smile disappeared. "Do whatever it takes to survive." He turned to Luxi. "I want you both in one piece."

Leto nodded and set his hands on his blade hilts.

Luxi looked up at him. "Leto, he's a ghost — *all* ghost. Your weapons won't have any effect on him."

Leto smiled nastily. "Oh, I know."

The lift stopped. The four guards shifted uneasily.

The commanding officer turned to the guard closest to the panel. "What the hell just happened?"

The guard peered at the lift panel. "We've stopped somewhere between Bronze and Silver."

The door opened on darkness

The guard stared at open door. "I didn't know there was a floor here?"

The commander scowled. "Neither did I."

The gray-green uniformed ghost formed in the doorway and focused on Luxi. "Enjoy your little run?"

The guards stared at the open doorway, clearly seeing nothing. "What the hell is going on?"

"I don't know!"

"Do something!"

"I am doing something! The panel's not working!"

"Then do something else!"

Luxi clenched her fists and glared at the ghost. "Go away."

The ghost smiled. "Oh, but you have something I need."

Amun took hold of Luxi's shoulder. "Luxi . . ." He looked toward the door and drew in a breath. "Blood and hell . . ."

Leto closed his hand tight on Luxi's other shoulder. "You can't have her."

The ghost focused on Leto. His eyes narrowed. "You . . ."

Leto bared his teeth in something that didn't even remotely resemble a smile. "Yeah, me."

The ghost tilted his head and his gaze focused on Luxi. "This lift is a rather large number of floors from ground level." He smiled. "Shall I drop it?"

The lights flickered in the lift and the floor shuddered. The guards shouted in alarm.

Luxi grabbed onto Leto to keep from falling. "No! Don't"

The ghost smiled. "Then come along, so they can get on with their . . . lives."

Leto's lips curled back from his teeth. "You bastard!"

The ghost grinned and his eyes narrowed. "You can come, too, if you'd like to be consumed." His gaze slid to Amun, braced next to Leto and clinging to Luxi's other shoulder. "In fact, you can bring your other companion as well."

Amun smiled slightly. "Thank you, but I'll pass." He

released Luxi's shoulder and stepped back.

Leto looked back at Amun.

Amun's mouth tightened.

The ghost shrugged. "Shall we proceed?"

Leto squeezed her shoulder.

Luxi wrapped her arms around herself and stepped toward the ghost with Leto at her side.

The ghost backed away from the doorway.

"Hey!" The guard commander moved toward them. "You can't get off here!"

Leto and Luxi stepped off.

The lift door closed with blinding speed, leaving them in utter darkness. Hollow bangs came from the other side of the door and faded.

"Alone at last." The ghost's voice was an icy wind.

Electronics hummed, and archaic lights flickered on directly overhead. Several popped and went out, but enough stayed on to show an enormous and empty oval-shaped room. Plain steel girders rose along the curved walls and arched upward. The far walls were enshrouded in darkness.

Luxi looked around. "Where are we?"

"Somewhere private." The ghost smiled. "Where I can feed without disturbance."

Luxi jerked back around to stare at the ghost. Icy shivers slid down her spine.

The ghost nodded slowly. "Oh yes, I'm afraid it's time."

Leto casually strode toward the ghost. "Out of sheer curiosity, are you from Terra, say about the turn of the nineteenth century?"

The ghost stilled. "I am."

Leto nodded. "I thought I recognized the uniform." He smiled and shook his head. "You are quite an old boy."

The ghost narrowed his eyes. "Far older than you."

Leto bit his lip and looked up at the girders overhead.

"Well, yes and no." He turned back to the ghost. "You see I was born at the turn of the twenty-second century, but I didn't actually lose all my biological components till centuries later. You've been dead longer than I have, but I was alive a lot longer than you."

The ghost scowled. "I had a living host . . ."

Leto shook his head. "Not quite the same thing." His raised his chin. "Oh, and for the record. You are not feeding on Luxi." He grinned. "She's my dinner date."

The ghost unsheathed his sword and knife. "Do you honestly think you can stop me?"

"Blades?" Leto rolled his eyes dramatically while pushing Luxi back. "You're using blades? Where's your imagination?"

The ghost froze and his brows lowered, clearly at a loss.

Leto laughed. "Oh please . . . You and I have been around long enough to know that true spirit-beings don't need weapons when we fight." He lifted his chin, and his body froze in place. Darkness shimmered around him, and then a black form stepped forward, out of the cyborg shell.

Leto's phantom body was shaped exactly the same, but he consisted of boiling black shadow with a gleam of scarlet flame for eyes. His long mane floated behind him in smoky tendrils. The shimmer of tiny lights, like blinking circuitry, winked throughout his form. He spread his arms wide and his fingers extended into claws as long as his forearm. "Real phantoms are weapons, all by themselves."

Luxi shivered under the impact of her talent. Leto's ghostly voice was a cool insinuating autumn wind with a hint of smoke, compared to the ghost's dead of winter chill.

The ghost stepped back, and his lips pulled back from his teeth. "Demon!"

Leto laughed. "You have no idea." He began to expand and reshape into a monstrous two-legged form of boiling winking shadow that was all claws, serrated scales and fangs. "Shall we dance?" He dropped to all fours and charged, his shape flowing into something resembling a scaled feline, complete with lashing tail.

The ghost danced out of reach and slashed out with his sword.

Leto moved under and around the blade like smoke. He laughed. "Oh, come on! You're supposed to be a badass! Let's see it!"

"Impudent fool!" The ghost whirled away and sheathed his blades. "Very well . . ." He clapped his hands together and snarled out a phrase Luxi's interpreter couldn't translate. He shouted and spread his hands.

His form extended up and up in a serpentine column of white smoke. A narrow muzzle formed, split and filled with teeth. Eyes of yellow flame opened. Scales and serrated fins emerged down the creature's spine. Clawed arms, legs, and wings, spread from its back. A long tail lashed, and it floated.

Leto laughed. "That's better!" Clawed wings spread from his monstrous feline form and he rose into the air. "Now we can do this properly . . ." He lunged, a snarling demonic creature of black smoke edged with flame.

CHAPTER FIFTEEN

Ethereal wind howled and screamed as the two monstrous ghosts entangled and lashed around each other, their battle filling the echoing room with their whirling storm of smoke. Leto's blackness flowed between shapes. Heads formed and bit from every conceivable angle. Clawed limbs formed and slashed from random places, and scarlet eyes opened everywhere.

The ghost remained solidly as a snarling and coiling white-winged serpent.

Luxi backed hard against the lift, her heart slamming painfully in her chest. The hurricane of power unleashed by the two spirits was horrifically terrifying. And yet the most fantastic thing she'd ever seen.

The lift door opened at her back.

Luxi screamed and whirled around.

Amun smiled at her. "Luxi! Where's Leto?"

Luxi pointed a shaking finger toward the center of the room.

Amun focused on Leto's abandoned cyborg body and frowned. "Why is he so still?"

Luxi had to take a breath to speak. "Because he's not in it."

Amun frowned. "What?"

"See for yourself." Luxi caught his hand, allowing him direct access to her talent.

Amun froze, staring. "Holy Mother Night!"

Someone came forward from within the lift. "May I see?"

Amun stepped from the lift and to the side, his hand nearly

crushing Luxi's fingers as he stared at the battling phantoms.

A young man, about a head shorter than Amun and dressed entirely in black, stepped from the lift. His broad shoulders and narrow waist were accentuated by his understated but exceedingly well-cut ankle-length suit coat and knife-edge dress slacks. His face had a handsomely exotic cast with straight black brows. His straight black hair was pulled back into a long tail that fell between his shoulder blades. He folded his hands behind his back. "I see." He inclined his head toward Amun then looked down at Luxi. "Which one is yours?"

Luxi stared into his shadow-filled eyes and shivered. *Great maker, another ghost!* "Leto is the black one."

The young man's almond-shaped eyes crinkled at the corners with his smile. "You must be Gentle-fem Emory."

Amun tore his gaze from the battling phantoms. "Luxi, this is Avatar Shido from the Temple of the Black Lotus."

Luxi grabbed onto Amun's wrist. "Another Avatar, like Vincent?"

Amun patted her hand. "Avatar Shido is nothing like Vincent. When I told him of your pursuer, he had no idea who Vincent was. Vincent is not an actual Avatar. He's a renegade."

"Oh, Vincent is an Avatar. He has a ghost." Shido shook his head. "However, the ghost is very much a renegade."

Amun looked back toward the phantoms and squeezed Luxi's hand. "Avatar Shido is here to collect the ghost."

Luxi looked over at Avatar Shido. "What about Vincent?"

"My associates already have him in custody." Shido sighed. "We'll see that he doesn't bother you anymore." He looked up at the battling spirits and stepped away from them. "I think this has gone on quite long enough." He pressed his palms together. "Tsuke."

A form stepped out of Avatar Shido's body and became a

broad man in overlapping decorative armor.

Shido turned to him. "Tsuke, do you recognize him?"

The broad ghost folded his arms across his armored chest. "I've never seen the young black one before. However, I am fairly certain the other is Yamura Kato."

Shido's hands closed into fists. "Bind-master Kato? He's been missing since Serendipity!"

"It wears his seal." Tsuke nodded toward Shido then focused on Luxi. "Oh, that's why he was chasing the little fem."

Shido folded his arms and raised his brow. "Pity she's claimed, yes?"

Tsuke smiled. "A very great pity."

Shido tilted his head toward the room. "Can you take Kato?"

Tsuke snorted. "In my sleep." He bowed to Shido then grinned and bowed to Luxi, too. He turned toward the center of the room and dissolved into a snaking mist that headed straight for the combatants.

The two battling ghosts snapped apart.

Tsuke slid between Leto and the flying serpent. "Good fight, boy. I'll take over from here."

Leto coalesced into his scaled feline form. "Are you sure you can handle him alone?"

"Of course! Kato and I are old companions." Tsuke laughed. "Go before you fall apart."

The flying serpent focused on the coiling mist. "Yoshiro Tsuke?"

The mist spread in a curtain of long fingers. "Yamura Kato. It is time to go home, binder. Your temple has missed you."

"No!" Kato screamed and attacked—and became entangled in Tsuke's web.

Tsuke's laughter boomed around the struggling serpent. "You know you cannot defeat me. Why do you try?"

Leto drifted toward his abandoned cyborg shell, his form

shrinking and fading until he was once again in a man's form.

Amun and Luxi hurried to meet him.

Leto dropped to the deck and stepped into his body. The cyborg gasped and collapsed to his knees. "Damn, I'm burnt."

Amun caught one arm and helped him onto his feet. "Are you going to live?"

Leto smiled tiredly. "Very funny. Ha, ha."

Luxi lifted his other arm over her shoulder and grinned at Amun. "He'll live."

Amun steadied Leto with a hand pressed to his heart. "Are you hurt?"

Leto leaned against Amun and shook his head. "I'm all right, just really exhausted."

Shido came up behind him. "You are lucky he didn't consume you."

"I think that was his plan." Leto turned to look at Shido. "But *my* plan was to keep him too busy to try it."

Shido nodded and smiled. "A good plan."

Leto raised his brow at Amun. "The specialist?"

Amun smiled tightly. "There is only one way to catch an Avatar, with another Avatar. This is Avatar Shido . . ."

"Shido!" Tsuke's voice boomed around them. "Kato is missing a part. I can't hold him for long without it!"

Luxi flinched. She was wearing it. "I have it."

All three men blinked. "You?"

Luxi felt her cheeks heat. "It's . . . I . . ." She swallowed. "I'm going to need help getting it off."

Shido nodded. "Show me."

Luxi ducked behind Leto. "No! It's . . ." She looked at Leto and Amun. "It's someplace private."

"Ah." Shido cleared his throat but couldn't quite conceal his amusement. "You have his cord, I assume?"

Heat scorched Luxi's cheeks. She nodded.

Amun frowned then turned to Luxi. "A cord?"

Shido turned to Amun. "She is going to need help getting it off."

Leto grinned. "I think I know what's going on. Luxi, why don't you show us in the lift?"

Luxi nodded.

Within the lift, Leto crouched down against the steel wall with Amun at his shoulder. Luxi parted her filthy and battered silk robes and turned around to show them the pair of red phantom cords that wound around her waist. From a knot over her navel, a pair of cords dropped straight down to a knot directly on her clit. After the knot, the cords bisected to frame her clit before traveling back up the seam of her butt cheeks to another knot at the small of her back.

Leto chuckled. "I'll be damned . . ."

Amun set his hand on Luxi's shoulder and frowned. "I've never seen anything like that."

Leto raised a brow. "I have, but not for a long time. Turn around Luxi. I'll get it off."

Luxi turned around to face the interior of the lift and looked over her shoulder. "You've seen this before?"

Amun frowned. "Why is she wearing it?"

Leto's fingers tugged at the knot in the back. "This little piece of work is something from Terra's very distant past. It's used to make the wearer very aroused, very fast." His fingers slid under and along the rope. Her cream slicked his fingers. He chuckled. "And it feels like it's doing its job pretty well, too."

Luxi flinched. "Just get it off."

Amun glanced at Luxi. "Is it uncomfortable?"

Luxi bit her lip. "No, just . . . um . . ." It was just driving her insane with lust, and Leto's inquisitive explorations were not making it any easier. She had to work to keep her breathing steady, to hide the moans that were dying to come out.

Leto gently drew the cord free of Luxi's crotch. "It's not supposed to be uncomfortable." He turned her around to work the knot from her waist. "It's supposed to be stimulating." He grinned at Amun. "Stimulating to both participants."

Amun raised a calculating brow. "You don't say?"

"The idea is to slide between the cords. The knots stimulate the wearer." Leto licked his lips. "While making the fit snug."

Amun pursed his lips. "How very interesting."

Leto tugged the cord free of her waist. "This is one wet rope."

Fine, rub it in. Luxi glared at him. "Get rid of it."

Leto laughed and tossed it. The phantom cord disappeared into thin air.

Luxi began to tug her rumpled robes back down.

Leto's slid his hands up the outside of her bare thighs. "Speaking of stimulating, I'm hungry." He looked up at Luxi with burning eyes. "How about a taste of that wet pussy?"

Luxi swallowed and clutched at her spread robes. "Right now?"

Leto licked his lips and focused on her exposed crotch. "I could really use it."

Luxi's heart hammered in her chest, and her breath hitched. She could use the relief, actually. "Um . . ."

Leto flashed a grin. "That wasn't a 'no.' Put your hands on the wall over my head and spread for me."

Luxi released her robes, letting them fall over Leto's arms. "But Avatar Shido will be in here . . ."

"So?" Leto tugged on her thighs. "You've had an audience before."

Luxi tipped forward, and her hands slapped against the wall as she arched over Leto's head.

Amun chuckled. "Lord Bel did mention something to that effect."

Luxi groaned. "Does everybody know?" Wet heat stroked

her inflamed flesh and lightning stuck. She gasped and shuddered.

"Mmm . . . Blood and hell, you're wet." He lapped loudly. "Close, too."

Glory, yes she was . . . Luxi came up on her toes, bucking in time to his lashing tongue. Tension built to a murderous pitch with incredible speed. She threw back her head and whimpers escaped her lips.

Amun came up behind her. "Is there room for one more?" His hands closed on Luxi's shoulders.

And a telepathic connection opened between them all. Heat and hunger washed in a tidal wave across the connection.

Amun gasped. "Great Maker . . ." His hands slid down and into Luxi's white robe to cup her breasts, his fingers closed on her swollen nipples and tugged.

Luxi arched, pressing her breasts deeper into Amun's hands, feeling his erection pressing against her butt. She turned to look up at him.

Amun took her mouth in a swift hungry kiss.

She moaned into his mouth. Amun shifted behind her and she felt him shifting his silver robes then moving her robes to one side to expose her butt. The heat of Amun's shaft slid between her thighs and up against her wet cunt, and Leto's working mouth.

Leto moaned in interest.

Amun gasped. "Just who are you licking?"

Luxi jolted with the echo of Amun's pleasure as Leto stroked the head of his cock with his wet tongue.

Leto chuckled. "What does it feel like?" His hands shifted under Luxi.

Luxi felt the head of Amun's cock center between her folds. She could actually feel both Leto's warm grasp around Amun's cock and Amun's desperate trembling need to thrust.

She could also sense his hesitation. She took a breath. "Amun, do it."

Amun thrust. His cock stretched and filled her with his hot, hard heat.

Luxi groaned.

Leto chuckled. "Oh yeah . . . fuck her." His mouth descended to where their bodies were joined. He lashed across her clit and the base of the hard cock lodged in her.

Amun groaned, withdrew and thrust, and thrust, and thrust . . . his hips slamming against her butt with merciless strength.

Luxi braced her feet against the slapping impact.

Leto's hands on her thighs steadied her.

Amun's fingers tightened on her aching nipples.

Climax rose and crested with breathless speed.

Leto groaned. "Oh . . . shit . . ." He pulled one hand away from her legs but continued his frantic licking.

Luxi couldn't see it, but she heard Leto open his suit. An echo of sensation told her that he had his cock out and was stroking it hard.

Leto pulled back, breathless. "Get down," he gasped. "Both of you, on your knees. Keep her upright."

Amun caught Luxi around the hips and pulled her down to her knees with him. Her thighs splayed wide. "Lean back against my shoulder."

Luxi set her head back against Amun's shoulder and put her arms up around his neck.

Amun smiled. "Yes, that's it." He thrust hard.

Leto stood and leaned back against the wall, stroking his heavy cock, his eyes gleaming with red flame. "Keep fucking, don't stop."

Amun pulled her robe open on top, baring her breasts. And thrust hard, up into her, hammering her with his strong strokes.

Luxi writhed, burning and on fire, her core clenching tight. Small gasping cries escaped her lips. She was going to cum . . .

Leto leaned over them, setting his hand on Amun's shoulder for balance and stroking his cock with vicious haste. "Oh, Maker, she's right there." He choked. "Give me your eyes!"

They both looked up.

Lightning struck and release exploded through all three of them. The liquid fire of rapture washed through them, and over them, each release flowing through each of them in a triple wave of intense burning pleasure. They howled, shuddered and bucked under the torment.

Leto's eyes burned — and pulled.

A part of Amun and Luxi was pulled, fluttering from within their hearts. They gasped.

Leto drew it in on a breath . . . and fed.

A stream of hot white viscous liquid splattered across Luxi's breasts, even as she felt the pulse of Amun's cock filling her.

Leto groaned and emptied stream after stream of hot cum. He exhaled and dropped to his knees, wrapping them both in his arms. He covered Luxi's mouth in a devouring kiss then turned to take Amun's.

They held each other, all three locked in a mutual embrace, trembling while the last of their shared pleasure burned down to embers.

Leto leaned back on his heels and grinned. "Oh, that was a nice snack."

Luxi groaned, feeling hot cum slithered down into her robes. "Glory, I'm covered in . . ." She narrowed her eyes at one, and then the other grinning male.

Amun choked out a laugh. "Cum. You are covered in Leto's cum." He pulled her robe back over her sticky breasts.

Leto chuckled. "And let me tell you, I was happy to put it there."

"You would be." Luxi writhed. "Bloody Fate, Amun, you're getting it all over the robes!"

Leto climbed to his feet and leaned against the side of the lift and laughed. "It's all over the robes anyway, I wasn't exactly careful."

Luxi shot him a hot look. "I noticed."

Amun snorted and pushed Luxi up on her feet. "The robes were already well beyond cleaning."

Luxi stood on shaky feet and felt more cum slithering down her thighs. "Oh, icky!"

Amun chuckled climbed to his feet. "Shall I run you a bath?"

Excitement coiled up Luxi's spine. "A real one, with water, in that huge tub?"

Amun smiled, tucking his robes back around him. "I'll even add bubbles."

Leto grabbed the front of Amun's robes and tugged him closer. "What do you say we all have a nice soak in the tub and spend the rest of the night fucking?"

Amun smiled. "That sounds very . . . appetizing."

CHAPTER SIXTEEN

"Is it safe to come in now?" Avatar Shido's voice was distinctly amused.

Luxi groaned and her cheeks flushed with warmth.

Amun chuckled. "Yes, we are quite finished."

Shido laughed as he stepped into the lift. "I'll have you know that Tsuke is quite upset that he wasn't invited." He turned and set his palm on the lift controls.

The doors closed, and the lift activated.

Leto pulled both Amun and Luxi into his embrace. He smiled but narrowed his eyes at the Avatar. "Sorry, private party."

Shido grinned. "That's what I told him." He tilted his head. "You're nearly back up to full strength. Your two chosen must be quite talented."

Leto relaxed against the back of the lift wall, an arm around Luxi and an arm around Amun. "That's one way to put it."

Amun lifted his chin and his brow. "I am a professional grade telepath."

Shido frowned thoughtfully. "Yes, Lord Amun, this I know, but according to my . . . impressions, the gentle-fem is also a major talent. In fact, her ghost-touch registers as being secondary, almost minor by comparison."

Amun gently pressed his fingers against Luxi's lips. "You are quite correct. Luxi is possessed of a major talent."

Luxi looked up at Amun in curiosity. Amun didn't want Shido to know about her fortunetelling abilities? How strange.

Shido's brows lifted. "I see." He focused on Luxi. "Should you ever be in need of employment, gentle-fem, the Temple of the Black Lotus would love to have you." He quoted a salary big enough to afford a small luxury cruiser.

Leto stilled utterly.

Amun frowned. "That is quite a *'princely'* sum, Avatar."

Shido smiled. "For a talent like hers? I can afford it."

Amun bit his lip and looked down at Luxi. "Would you prefer to go with Avatar Shido?"

Luxi frowned up at Amun. "But I thought I was . . ." *Indentured, a legal slave.*

Amun smiled, a little sadly. "That can be changed, easily in fact."

Leto brushed his fingers across her brow. "Luxi, if you don't want to stay, we're not going to make you."

Amun glanced at Leto then looked at Luxi. "Would you like to . . . go?"

Luxi grabbed her elbows and blinked rapidly to control the stinging in her eyes. Didn't they want her anymore? She took a deep breath. "If you don't need me . . . to stay . . ."

"What kind of question is that?" Leto frowned. "If we didn't want you, we wouldn't have offered in the first place."

Amun leaned close to catch her hand. "Actually, I'd prefer to keep you if you don't mind?"

"You would?" Luxi bit her lip as her heart constricted in her chest. They wanted her?

Amun smiled. "Of course, we haven't had a chance to explore the full range of your . . ." He raised a red brow and gave her a thoroughly lascivious smile. "Talents, yet."

Leto glared down at her. "Yes, we want you. Is that clear enough?"

Luxi had to remember to breathe. "Oh . . . I . . ." They wanted her to stay — with them. "I'd like to stay if you don't mind?"

Amun nodded and smiled broadly. "Good."

Leto's head fell back against the lift wall. "Thank the Maker!"

Luxi turned to look over at Avatar Shido. "I'm sorry Avatar, but I'm going to have to turn your more than generous offer down."

Shido grinned and shrugged. "I understand perfectly."

Leto smiled down at her. "I was beginning to think you didn't like us anymore."

"Of course I like you!" Luxi rolled over to wrap Leto in a hug. She turned and smiled at Amun. "I like you both a lot." She rubbed her chest against Leto's silk court robe, just a little.

Leto looked down and raised a brow. "You're rubbing cum all over me."

Luxi looked up and grinned. "Why, yes, I am."

Amun choked on a chuckle. "Well, since you are remaining my employee, so to speak, you realize you'll have to be punished for ruining that expensive robe he's wearing?"

Luxi's mouth fell open. "Punished?"

Luxi crossed her arms over her naked breasts and stared. The huge black and gold marble bathtub was filled nearly to the brim with steaming bubbles. It looked completely inviting. She scowled. "Guys, this is grossly unfair."

"Unfair?" Leto let the sleek black dressing robe slide from his bare shoulders and tossed it on the counter. "I don't think so at all!" He turned to face her. His erection was a pale smooth column arching rigidly up to his navel. "I was all for a spanking, myself."

Luxi's core gave a hungry wet throb. He looked good enough to eat. Then it registered as to what he'd just said. "A spanking?"

Amun smiled at Leto as he let his pale silver robe slide off. "Would you prefer a spanking?" He set his robe on the counter over Leto's.

"No, but . . ." Luxi dragged her gaze from Leto's ruggedly masculine body and mouthwatering cock, only to find Amun's sleek muscular form and rigid cock just as arresting. She had to take a breath and close her eyes against the sight before she could gather her thoughts enough to deliver her answer. "Look, I didn't mind taking a shower to get all the dirt off before I got in the tub, but I just got that stupid rope off . . ." She opened her eyes and pointed toward the cream cords bound around her waist and crotch. "And you put another one on me?"

Leto shrugged. "We had to do something to punish you."

Luxi's mouth fell open. "What?"

Amun set his hands on her shoulders and smiled from only a kiss away. "Think of it as therapy; to get past your traumatic experience."

Leto strode past them chuckling. "You two can talk, I'm getting in the tub." He climbed the three steps up and stepped over the tub's broad edge then down into the water. He groaned. "Blood and hell, this feels good."

Amun turned Luxi toward the deep tub. "Go on."

Luxi stared longingly at the bubbles. "But the cord is going to get all wet . . ."

Leto grinned as he moved through the waist-deep water. "Yes, and slippery, too. That's high-quality silk you know." He sat and turned to sit on an underwater seat and leaned against the back with a heartfelt moan.

Luxi groaned. *Oh, what the hell . . .* She stepped to the edge, the cords caressing and rubbing, the small knot shifting back and forth against her clit with her movements. A flare of erotic heat coiled and clenched deep in her core. Carefully, she stepped up and over, then into the foamy water, sinking up to her breasts. The warmth caressed her deliciously with just a hint of sting. A moan of raw pleasure escaped her.

Amun followed right behind her then gently steered her

toward Leto, their strides sloshing through the bubbles.

Leto lifted his arms and his smile turned distinctly lascivious. "Come sit in my lap, little girl."

Luxi raised her brow disdainfully.

"Go on." Amun gave Luxi a little push.

Luxi yelped and tipped forward, catching onto Leto's shoulders . . . and felt the moving darkness under his skin. Her hands opened wide, spreading her fingers to feel more of him.

"Come down here." Leto groaned, caught her around the waist and tugged her down and across his lap.

Luxi splashed into the sudsy heat, her legs splayed over his right knee and her right arm around Leto's neck for balance. The heated water closed over her breasts in a rich decadent blanket of scented warmth. She groaned and released his neck to fall back, arching and stretching, luxuriating in the sinful delight of a bath. Her red curls fanned out in the water.

Leto raised his arm to support her neck, keeping her face out of the water, and laughed. "I think she likes it." He grinned at Amun.

Luxi grinned. "I love water."

Amun smiled and sank into the water. "It certainly looks that way." He scooted up against Leto's right shoulder and lifted Luxi's legs over his lap. He smiled at Leto. "I am interested in just how slippery that silk is getting."

Leto raised his brow. "Then why don't you check and see?" He licked his lips.

Amun smiled and leaned closer. "Don't mind if I do." He slid his hand languorously up Luxi's inner thighs and parting them.

Luxi shivered. "Amun?"

Leto bent down and caught Luxi's chin. "Kiss me."

Luxi leaned up, opening for his kiss. Velvet softness moved against her lips. She stroked his full bottom lip with the tip of her tongue then extended her tongue to meet his. Warmth, wetness, breath, shadows . . .

Amun's fingers drifted higher up her thighs. He brushed against the plump outer lips and then the intimate folds of her core, drawing small shudders from her flesh.

Leto pressed closer and his tongue surged into her mouth for a thorough exploration. His hand closed on her breast and squeezed. His thumb rubbed, circling one swollen pink nipple, sending jolt after hot jolt straight to Luxi's clit.

Luxi shivered with growing anticipation.

Amun's fingers lightly brushed the cords. "This is getting quite slippery." He pressed against the silk rope framing her clit.

Lightning speared Luxi's tender clit. She moaned into Leto's mouth.

Amun slid two fingers between the silk cords and into her warmth.

Luxi broke the kiss on a gasp and rolled against Amun's fingers. "Oh . . . shit!" Wet heat clenched tight in her belly

"I see what you meant about 'snug'." Amun swept his thumb over the point of her clit.

Luxi bucked hard.

"And effective." Amun smiled.

Leto grinned and tugged on Luxi's trapped nipple. "If I'd had more cord, I could have done the same to her breasts too."

Amun licked his lips. "Ah, then we will most definitely have to invest in more silk cord."

Luxi shivered under their hands. "Haven't you done enough?" The fire in her tormented nipple and pressured clit were building a ferocious and ravenous ache in her belly. If they kept this up, she was going to cum right there . . .

Leto grinned as he squeezed and tugged Luxi's breast and nipple. "Are you kidding? With enough silk rope, I could suspend you in any position I wanted." He looked over at Amun.

"It was a hobby of mine at one time, suspending captives."

Amun raised a brow thoughtfully. "That sounds quite entertaining."

"Especially on a long voyage." Leto grinned.

Luxi groaned, under the pleasurable torment of their stirring hands. Being tied up and pleasured by the both of sounded like a very delicious idea, but she wasn't sure if it was the brightest idea in the cosmos. Glory only knew what they'd think to do with her and to her . . .

Amun reached up to cup her other breast then trapped her nipple in his fingers. "How much rope would be needed, for such a suspension?" He pinched the swollen point.

Luxi gasped. Erotic fire seared through her shoving her right on the edge of a ferocious release. The climax slid back and she bucked helplessly in reaction.

Leto chuckled as Luxi thrashed in his arms. "I can give you an exact set of lengths and diameters if you like."

Amun grinned. "I'd like."

Luxi panted and boiled, shivering under the ravages of her close brush with release. "I don't know if I want to be suspended."

Amun pulled his fingers from her core and pressed them to her lips. "Suck."

Luxi opened her mouth and took his fingers into her mouth, tasting her own cream on her tongue. She shivered. It was so . . . *naughty.*

Amun pressed his fingers against his tongue. "Luxi, you are the indentured employee, and I am your master. You will take your orders like a good employee. Yes?" He pulled his finger from her mouth.

Luxi stared at him in shock. "But I thought you could remove . . . that?"

Amun smiled. "Yes, I can. But alas, for you, I am no longer so inclined."

"What?" Luxi struggled to sit up. "Oh, you . . ."

Leto held her down grinning. "Controlling bastard?"

Amun shook his head. "Leto did warn you that I have control issues."

"I did." Leto nodded, not even bothering to hide his grin. "Luxi, I did tell you."

Luxi folded her arms over her breasts and glared at them both.

Amun blinked. "Is that a pout?"

Leto stuck out his bottom lip in imitation. "Don't you love us anymore?"

Luxi opened her mouth . . . and couldn't say a word. *Love?* Shock rippled through her entire body and a fist squeezed around her heart, stealing her breath. Actually . . . she did. She did love them. *Oh Glory . . .* How had that happened?

Amun frowned. "Luxi, what is it?"

It took two tries before she could get enough air to breathe. "I, uh . . ." A shudder raked her. "Actually, I think, I do."

Leto stilled. "You do?"

Luxi turned away and nodded. She was in love — with both of them. And they were in love — with each other. She had to close her eyes, but it didn't stop the ache in her heart, or in her eyes. It hurt . . . Glory it hurt, to be on the outside.

Amun glanced at Leto and tugged Luxi's hands free of her arms. Leto released her to let Amun draw her into his arms. "Luxi, it's going to be all right."

Luxi closed her arms around Amun's neck. "I'm sorry."

"Sorry?" Leto shifted closer to Amun to catch her gaze. "For what?"

Amun stroked her back. "Luxi we don't mind if you love us."

"Oh, hell no, we don't mind!" Leto tugged at her fingers. "Luxi, do you have any idea how hard it is to find someone that would?"

Luxi sniffed and smiled. "I didn't have any problems."

Leto grinned. "That's because you're as odd as we are."

"Odd?" Amun turned to frown at Leto. "And what do you mean by that remark?"

Leto shook his head and grinned. "Oh, come on, a telepath, a cyborg and a fortuneteller? It sounds like the beginning of a very bad joke."

Amun gently disengaged Luxi from around his neck. "Is that so?"

Luxi shifted away, watching in interest.

Leto slid away from Amun. "Amun, what's going on in that head of yours?"

Amun smiled and his eyes narrowed. "Luxi, would you like to help me tie Leto down to the bed?"

Leto's mouth fell open. "What?"

Luxi grinned. "I think I would like that a lot."

Leto glanced at Luxi, his eyes wide. "Luxi!" He looked at Amun and moved further away. "What about the bath?"

Amun rose from the bath seat. "It will still be here when we're done. The heaters will keep it warm." Amun smiled as he stalked toward Leto. "Luxi, fetch the towels."

Luxi grinned as she sloshed toward the edge of the tub. "Coming right up!"

Leto backed away from Amun. "Amun you're not serious?"

"Leto, are you going to come quietly?" Amun licked his lips. "Or do I need to use the override codes on you?"

Leto stilled. "You wouldn't . . ."

CHAPTER SEVENTEEN

"Luxi, are you done?"

Down on her knees at the foot, and on the left side of Amun's massive bed, Luxi finished tying the scarlet robe tie around the iron bed support. She tugged at the half-hitch knot making sure it was tight. It was a secure knot, but it would come free with one quick tug. "Yes, it's done!"

"Good, come on up on the bed."

Luxi shoved her long hair, still damp from the bath, back from her cheek, and rose from her knees. The black marble and silver master bedroom was softly lit by a half-dozen small frosted glass domes scattered around the room. The black velvet drapes had been drawn all the way back to the head of the monstrous bed.

Leto was a pale sculpture of erotic masculine perfection spread out across the cream sheets in the center of the bed. His unbound silver hair gleamed as it spilled across the black brocade pillow under his head. His cock was a stiff ivory length arching above his belly. He was tied, wrist and ankle, to the four corners of the bed with every robe tie and curtain cord Amun could get his hands on.

Leto twisted his bound hands, and glared at Amun, kneeling between his spread legs. "There's not a whole lot I can do from this position."

"Of course not." Amun grinned broadly, his hands resting in his naked hips. His long, deep blood mane felt in a rich cloak down his back. "That *is* the idea, Leto."

Luxi climbed onto the bed and crawled on hands and knees

toward the men. Both of them looked good enough to eat. The cords that still bound her rubbed against her tender inner lips and clit enticingly.

Amun turned to regard her with his bright green eyes, then held out his hand. "Come over here, Luxi."

Luxi took his hand and rose up on her knees at his side. "What are we going to do now?"

"Now?" Amun leaned closer to brush a soft kiss on her lips. "We're going to fuck Leto."

Luxi frowned *"We* are?"

"Yes, *we* are." Amun smiled down at Leto and pointed to a white squeeze tube lying above Leto's pillow. "Hand me the gel."

Leto shifted on the bed. "Amun what are you up to?"

Luxi leaned over to get the tube of gel, somewhat confused. The gymnastics of what Amun was saying didn't quite match up in her mind. She turned back to Amun and handed him the white tube.

"You heard me." Amun opened the gel, squeezed out a generous dollop onto his palm then rubbed his palms together.

Leto frowned. "But I thought you wanted to try Luxi's binding?"

Luxi's head came up. This was news to her.

"Oh, I do." Amun grasped his cock with both hands. "Eventually." He sighed with pleasure.

Leto groaned. "Oh, you bastard . . ."

Amun smiled.

Luxi raised a brow. If Amun was using gel, then Amun was probably going up somebody's butt . . . She winced. *I hope that isn't for me.* Amun was way too big. They both were.

Leto shifted and his ties groaned. "It's damned hard for me to get off that way if I can't move."

Amun leaned down to kiss Leto's brow. "I'll make it up to

you." He closed the tube and set it down on the far side of the bed. He got up on his knees and straddled Leto's hips, his strong cock striking the side of Leto's cock. He turned and held out his hand. "Luxi, come to me."

Luxi eyed the two cocks, one slicked with lubrication gel, and one not, with grave suspicion. She reached out and grasped Amun's hand.

Amun tugged her close and turned her to face the head of the bed. He patted her thigh. "Up and over, you're riding on top."

Leto licked his lips and scowled. "Amun, I'm going to get you for this."

Luxi nibbled on her bottom lip and stood up on the mattress. She stepped over Leto's hips to straddle him.

Amun caught Luxi's hips and steadied her. "There, sit and take Leto into you."

Luxi came down on her knees and leaned forward over Leto's broad chest. She reached back between her thighs to grasp his heated shaft and stopped, staring at his pale, stiff nipples. She licked her lips.

Leto's brows shot up.

Luxi held his gaze, leaned to the right and licked the stiff nub with the tip of her tongue. The sensation of a second nipple right under it was overpowering. She pressed her entire mouth to his nipple and licked, exploring the odd but definitely interesting sensation with her lips and tongue, then sucked. She released his nipple with a wet smack.

Leto released a long, harsh groan and shifted under her. "I changed my mind. I'll cum just fine as long as Luxi keeps that up."

Amun chuckled. "Leto, you are such a little slut."

Leto lifted his head and grinned. "Hell yeah, I'm a slut!" He focused on Luxi. "Get that cock stuffed babe. I'm in the mood to fuck."

Get that cock stuffed? Luxi snorted. *I'll show you a stuffed cock.* She set her palm on his breast for leverage and leaned up a bit. She angled Leto's broad cockhead against the folds of her core—and encountered the cords.

"Allow me." Amun's warm thumbs parted the damp and slick silk cords. "Now."

The pressure of the cord's knot on her clit increased. Luxi groaned. She took a breath and rubbed Leto's cockhead against her slick folds, then shifted her knees back a little.

Leto closed his eyes and sucked in a breath. "Luxi I'm dying here . . . do it!"

Luxi shot Leto a glare. "You'll get it, don't rush me!"

"Oh, he'll get it." Amun laughed. "Go on, Luxi."

Luxi sat back, pressing his broad head into the snug hungry mouth of her core. As she progressed back and down, increment by increment, her body stretched to accommodate his girth.

Amun released the cords and they closed around Leto's cock.

Leto closed his eyes, sucked in a breath and bit his lip. "Oh, that's tight."

Luxi had nearly the full length in her when she stopped for a breath, slid up just a bit then came down hard, seating herself fully.

Leto gasped and his back arched, head tipped back, his hands balled into fists, his body straining up off the mattress. "Oh . . . shit . . ." He dropped.

Luxi levered herself up and smiled. "Better?"

Leto wheezed dramatically. "Much."

Amun choked out a laugh. "Good, my turn. Luxi, lean down, and torture Leto's nipples for a bit."

Luxi eyed Amun suspiciously and sucked on her bottom lip. "Okay." She turned to face Leto and leaned down, pressing her body against his long warm length. His cock moved deliciously within her.

Leto smiled. "I love it when you do that tongue thing."

Luxi grinned. "Good. How about the teeth thing?"

Leto's smile disappeared. "Teeth thing?"

Luxi pressed her mouth over his nipple to demonstrate. Her tongue flicked and licked the tender nub then she raked her teeth across it.

Leto groaned. "Oh . . . the teeth thing. Yeah, I like the teeth thing. Do that some more."

Behind her, Amun pressed a hand to Luxi's back, encouraging her to lay flat. He parted the cords and his finger pressed against the rose of her anus. It was slick with gel.

Luxi froze. "Amun?"

"Push out Luxi." His finger pressed insistently. "Push out hard."

Luxi took a deep breath and pushed out. His finger slid past her anal ring and invaded her. She groaned. "Amun, I really don't think . . ."

"Luxi, you are very tight. Has no one ever been here before?" His finger moved around within her, coating her interior with gel. "Keep pushing out Luxi, it relaxes the muscles."

Luxi whimpered. "No, I've never done it before." It didn't actually hurt, in fact, it was almost enjoyable, but the sensation was a dark and very different type of pleasure.

Amun rotated his finger within her. "Oh? Good." He pulled his finger back out.

Leto's brows shot up. "You've never had it up the ass?"

Luxi flinched. "No, I haven't." Glory, he made it sound like she was still virginal.

Amun leaned over her back and his hand closed on her shoulder. "Luxi, I need you to push out as hard as you can." The heat of his cock pressed against her anus.

Luxi cowered on top of Leto, and her heart beat in her throat. "Amun, you're too big."

Amun's fingers bit into her shoulder. "You'll adjust. Push, because I am coming in, right now." He pressed hard.

Luxi's anus spread under the pressure, and the sharp pain caught her off guard. She gasped. "It hurts!"

Amun smacked her butt. "Push out!"

Luxi whimpered and pushed. Her anus spread with a speed she didn't expect and swallowed Amun's cockhead. She groaned. "You're too big!"

Amun pulled on her shoulder and shoved his cock harder. "Keep pushing!"

Luxi kept pushing. Amun's cock was a hot bar of steel spreading her obscenely wide as it slid against Leto's cock already lodged within her. She moaned.

Amun groaned at her back. "Blood and hell, you are tight, woman!"

Leto chuckled under them. "I guess that mean's she's going to need fairly frequent anal reaming to loosen her up."

Luxi whimpered. "Leto, you are not helping!"

"Of course not." Leto cleared his throat. "I'm tied up at the moment."

Amun's thighs brushed hers, and he sighed. "There, I'm in."

Luxi released a tiny breath. "Great."

Amun leaned down over her, setting his hands on the mattress to either side. He kissed her shoulder. "Do you know how long it has been since I fucked a virgin ass?"

"I don't know, and I don't care!" Luxi shifted, trying to relieve the burning ache in her ass. "You guys are freaking huge!"

Leto grinned completely without shame. "What a nice thing to say."

Luxi scowled down at him.

Leto licked his lips. "Wait till it's my turn to ream your tight little butt."

"When we have her suspended from the bulkhead, there'll be plenty of opportunities." Amun groaned and began to withdraw.

Luxi gasped. The pain in her butt had transformed to something entirely different, almost pleasurable.

Leto shifted impatiently. "Amun, you're not linking us. I don't feel a thing."

Amun chuckled. "This is Luxi's first ass-fucking, are you sure you want it?"

"I like pain. Leto grinned. "Do me."

Amun stopped with only his cockhead left in Luxi's ass. "Done."

Sensation rushed over Luxi in a heavy wave of raw lust and erotic and fiery tightness. She could feel her body's wet heat tight around both of their cocks and her own wet ravenous hunger under it all.

Amun thrust hard, driving Luxi forward. As Amun's surged in, Leto's cock withdrew.

Sharp pain, erotic heat, brutal pleasure, fierce tightness . . .

They gasped.

Leto choked. "Oh, shit . . ."

Amun's arm closed tight around Luxi's waist. He pulled her back and down onto Leto's hard cock. His cock withdrew from her anal passage with a slow rich decadence that made them all groan and writhe with her pleasure.

Amun thrust, pushing Luxi forward and forcing Leto's withdrawal. The cocks rubbed against each other, one going in, and one coming out, with only a thin wall of flesh between them.

Luxi gasped, inundated by their extreme pleasure in her tight heat, underscored by the edge of pain from her anal reaming.

Amun's body damped with sweat. He stopped, fully within her. "Lean down and lick his nipples."

Luxi leaned down and took Leto's nipple into her mouth. She laved it with her tongue. The echo of Leto's pleasure fired her nipples as well.

Amun withdrew in a rich slide of dark delight.

Luxi sucked hard on Leto's nipple and bore down on Leto's cock in pure reaction.

Amun slammed into her, delivering sharp pain that mixed with the raw delight of surging into her tight, hot passage.

Luxi rose from Leto's cock and bit down on his nipple, bringing a different kind of pleasure and pain into the erotic mix.

Leto groaned and bucked under her, driven to seek more.

Amun withdrew more quickly.

Luxi surged down onto Leto's cock, filling her hungry core with his thick heat and feeling the echo of the cords rubbing and squeezing around Leto's cock. She moved to Leto's other nipple and took it into the wet heat of her mouth.

Amun surged in, bringing a rush of fire and power.

Luxi bit down on Leto's nipple, delivering a sharp spark that detonated in her nipple, her clit, and in Leto's cock, even as his cock slid from her body.

Burning thrust, heated withdrawal, and a hot wet tormenting mouth on a sensitive and tender nipple . . . The vicious delight of one washing into the mind of the next, and the next . . . The fierce ruthless ecstasy was underscored and brightened by the slight edge of pain. Over and over, and over . . .

Climax surged and crested in a blast-furnace of intensity.

Leto howled under them, ravenous and demanding.

Amun and Luxi stared into Leto's burning and hungry eyes.

Release crashed through them and took them in a fire fall of horrific glory.

Leto took — and they gave.

They screamed.

Luxi opened her eyes, her cheek pressed against the warmth of Leto's shoulder.

Leto smiled, his eyes hooded, and his expression sated. "Hey, love." He kissed her brow and his arms closed around her.

She frowned, confused, but unsure why.

Alongside Leto, Amun groaned and rolled onto his back. "That was . . . impressive."

Leto stretched. "Maker's balls, I haven't been this sated in over a century." He closed his arms around them both, his wrists trailing the bright ribbons of ripped robe ties. "And I didn't take either of you out."

Amun rolled up onto his side to throw his arm over Leto's waist. He smiled lazily. "That's because you have two major talents in bed."

Leto turned to look over at Luxi. "I'll say."

Luxi finally figured out what had caught her attention. "You broke the ties."

"What?" Leto lifted a wrist and then his ankle, both trailing shreds of robe ties. "Well, yeah. I'm a cyborg. Unless you use cabling wire, I'm going to snap it if I'm not careful."

"Oh, I forgot." Luxi sat up and groaned. Every muscle in her body ached.

"You forgot?" Leto blinked. How could you forget?"

"Hmm? Oh, it was easy." Luxi slid to the side of the bed and stood on wobbly legs. She padded gingerly around the end of the bed.

Amun dropped his head on Leto's shoulder and laughed tiredly. "She forgot you were a cyborg."

"Luxi? How could you forget?" Leto frowned ferociously. "And where are you going?"

"I keep forgetting because I don't see you that way." Luxi

turned back to the bed and smiled. "You don't kiss like a cyborg." She padded toward the bathroom. "I'm going back to the bubble bath to soak out some of these aches." Moments later, Luxi stepped into the blissfully hot water. She submerged to her neck, and the heat sank loosening fingers into her muscles. She groaned in delighted gratitude. The heaters had done their job and kept the water at the perfect temperature—just on the edge of hot.

Groans and the footfalls of bare feet announced Leto and Amun's arrival. Splashes and delighted moans followed soon after.

Leto leaned up against the side of the tub next to Luxi and sank until the water rose to his neck. He sighed. "This was a good idea."

Amun stationed himself on Luxi's other side and submerged to his neck as well. "Why do I have the feeling that we are going to need a lot of baths?"

Luxi smiled. "Because you are a man of rare intelligence?"

Amun grinned. "Keep that up and I'll give you a raise."

Leto's brows rose. "You mean she actually gets paid?"

Amun turned and smiled at Leto. "Are you sure you want to go there?"

Leto bit back his grin. "Now that I think about it? Not really. Maybe later?"

Amun turned to Luxi. "Are you sure you want to stay with us?"

Luxi yawned. "Yup." She smiled tiredly.

Leto and Amun traded grins.

Leto lifted his arms and folded them behind his neck. "Good, because I didn't want to have to hunt you down."

Luxi frowned at him. "You wouldn't . . ."

Amun rolled his eyes. "Oh, yes, he would. And he'd bring you back, too." He smiled slyly. "You'll give in simply to stop all the begging and pleading."

Leto turned and frowned at Amun. "Hey! I did not plead!"

Luxi rolled her eyes. "You two . . ."

"No, Luxi." Amun caught her chin and turned her to face him. "Us three." He pressed a gentle kiss to her lips.

Leto pressed against her side and took over where Amun's kiss left off.

ABOUT THE AUTHOR

Morgan Hawke

"For me, writing is more than a passion; it's an *obsession*. The stories crowd into my head. I write them down so I can get some peace. Where do I get my ideas? Rampant curiosity. I play the game of 'What If?' with everything I encounter. Everything I do and everything I see triggers a story to be told. I am a voracious reader of Romance, Science-Fiction, Fantasy, Horror, and Erotica, so naturally, my stories follow along the lines of what I like to read."

Morgan Hawke has lived in seven states of the US and spent two years in England. She has been an auto mechanic, a security guard, a waitress, a groom in a horse-stable, in the military, a copywriter, a magazine editor, a professional tarot reader, a belly-dancer and a stripper. Her personal area of expertise is the strange and unusual.

Ms. Hawke has been writing erotic fiction since 1998 and maintains a close and personal relationship with her computer and her cat.